RELAT

UNCERTAINTY

Alex Knibbs

Dedication

This book is simply dedicated to my 5 human 'guinea pigs' who willingly gave of their time and provided sufficient positive feedback to convince me of the viability of this project. Without their input it may not have been brought to fruition. They are: Deb, Hazel, Madi, Sarah and Tina. Thank you all for your kind words.

Contents

CHAPTER I

The present (Roughly 2018)

They were just an ordinary couple if there can ever be such a thing. Mike was 19 and Emma was 2 years younger. They had met a few years earlier in their mid-teens when they were both members of the local swimming club in Kendal, Cumbria. Mike had been a keen swimmer for most of his life, having been taught by his father when he was just 4 years old. To coin a phrase, he could swim like the proverbial fish, and it was fair to say he'd become a proficient and strong swimmer during his teenage years. He was never going to have made it to National honours, but he was certainly a very able and solid club swimmer, with a preference for swimming front crawl although he was more than competent on all strokes which also made him a tour de force on the more arduous individual medley events. Emma, in contrast, had gravitated to swimming when she was a little older, having savoured the temptations of hockey, tennis and swimming after she had joined her local secondary school when she was 11. For her, swimming was more a pleasurable pastime. Although she enjoyed swimming competitively, she felt a certain innate pleasure from simply being immersed in water. It was a place where not only could she maintain a decent level of physical activity and fitness, but also a place where she could ''lose herself', mentally, for a while. She had been moderately competitive but only insofar as that this was what had been expected of members at the club.

They had both been studious at school. Mike had shown a prowess for Geography and Business and had gained very respectable A levels in those two subjects, along with Economics that had enabled him to be offered several places at some quite prestigious Universities. Richard and Sue, Mike's parents, had been incredibly supportive of Mike and he was aware that they'd secretly hoped he might have followed in the medical family footsteps. Both Richard and his brother Dennis had studied medicine and become doctors. Dennis had chosen the path to become a Consultant Microbiologist at the local hospital, while Richard had become a general practitioner. While this had afforded Mike the opportunity to see first-hand what a life in medicine could be like he had also seen both sides of that dynamic. Certainly, both his father and uncle had done very well for themselves. They were financially well off and clearly appeared to enjoy their vocations, but Mike had also heard about, and witnessed first-hand, the challenges they'd both faced, especially during their early days: the extraordinarily long working hours that went on sometimes for weeks or even months at a time; the innate stress of having to sometimes make those 'life and death' decisions. Moreover. He was also aware of the occasional slice of luck needed to be in the right place at the right time to fulfil their career progression. Mike had weighed all of this up during his early teenage years. Ultimately, he simply did not feel he had that burning desire to take up medicine and his feeling was that that element needed to be rigidly fixed in place to warrant pursuing such a course. At the same time, he very much enjoyed the academic areas he had decided to pursue himself and reckoned that business in general could also prove to be both enjoyable and lucrative, in its own way.

1

It was a bit of a tough decision but ultimately, he had chosen the offer of a place at Loughborough to study Economics, in part because he had already been aware of the excellent sports facilities they had there, and he harboured a desire to at least continue competing in swimming through his undergraduate years. His dedication and perseverance seemed to be paying off as he had already got a solid first year under his belt and he was hoping that, with continued perseverance and diligence, his goal of graduating with a 2:1 was definitely in reach and, with the rub of the green, a First was in sight as a stretch goal. Ultimately, he already had visions of landing himself a role as a Trainee Business Analyst or similar. There was a large pharmaceutical company based not too far away in Cheshire and this was also at the back of his mind as a potential career path to follow.

Mike's family were also very much into sporting pursuits. Richard, his father, had also been a keen swimmer in his youth and had competed at County level. In addition, he was also a keen cross-country runner and, at one point he had also dabbled in modern pentathlon activities, although he found the rigors of fencing and pistol shooting somewhat more challenging and, as for the equestrian element, well, that had been his weaker discipline. Alas, these athletic extra-curricular activities had ultimately taken second fiddle as his academic activities began to take off. Unsurprisingly, as his career path as a physician took off, he found himself with less time to devote to such pursuits. In his late 20s he had got married and, soon afterwards, the patter of tiny feet effectively put paid to any return to his erstwhile sporting activities.

Dennis, somewhat similarly, was a very keen runner in his teenage years and he had also competed at County level. At one point he was vying for international selection but never quite made the grade. Like his brother, Richard, medical studies effectively took over and athletic endeavours took a back seat once he was in his early 20s. He still ran regularly, but it was as much to keep fit and conducted primarily at weekends.

Emma, too, had done well at school academically, although her choice of subjects studied at A level were more science based: she had chosen Biology, Chemistry and Psychology. A little like Mike, Emma, too, was applying herself well to the task and was hoping to achieve 3 'B' grades, which she felt would help her achieve her ambition of studying for a degree in nursing at Keele University. She still felt there was much work still to do as she looked towards starting her final year. Their burgeoning relationship had also, in part, factored into her choice of place to study. Keele had a solid reputation for Nursing but was also less than an hour's commute from where Mike was living in rented accommodation in a suburb of Macclesfield.

For Emma, her parents had also been supportive of her but, unlike Mike, there was no existing family vocational tradition for her to follow. Her mother, Linda, had been a PE teacher. Now aged 63, she had opted to take early retirement several years earlier. As far as Emma understood things, once she'd given birth to Emma in her early 40s, she taken off the statutory maternity time allowed to cope with Emma for a year. Although she had then returned to teaching PE, the challenge of giving birth coupled with the extra demands brought from bringing up a new infant – who then transitioned into becoming a toddler, convinced Linda that maybe she should consider taking the early retirement option. Her father, James, was a successful Senior Project Manager in a food manufacturing company and it was certainly Emma's impression as she'd been growing up that they could be considered comfortably well off, financially. Consequently,

Linda had decided to opt for a half-way house solution employment-wise and, when she was 45, she negotiated with her school to continue teaching PE on a part-time basis. That arrangement had lasted for a few more years until she was 50, at which point she decided to fully take the plunge to become officially retired. This had enabled her to take a fuller role in looking after Emma, where, previously, she had placed some reliance on a part-time child minder to oversee Emma when she'd been working. Unbeknown to Emma at the time, but on reflection, she realised that this had suited them both perfectly. Linda was then able to devote much of her time to Emma's continued upbringing. Emma, in turn, had the solidity of a robust family background where her mom was always on hand to provide the caring maternal support. In addition, there was then no need to employ the childminder and, even though this had only been needed on a part-time basis, it had nevertheless turned into an additional family cost saving.

James, her father, had, like Linda, also been caring and affectionate towards her as she was growing up, but, as most young girls know, the bond between a mother and a daughter, once forged, remains special for ever.

Theirs had been a traditional relationship that had begun as friendly acquaintances at the swimming club. When Mike was 17, he had summoned up the courage to ask her out to go ten pin bowling with him and, over the following few months their friendship grew and blossomed. Although mainly unspoken, they both felt that, at some point, assuming the relationship continued to evolve, it was likely that they would one day settle down together. Currently, they had fallen into a routine of meeting up most weekends, with Emma commuting up to Macclesfield on a Friday evening to spend a couple of days with Mike before travelling back to Keele on the Sunday evening.

In terms of overall family dynamics, Mike and Emma found they got on extremely well with each other's parents. Mike was a naturally ebullient, fun-loving individual and making new acquaintances seemed to come quite naturally to him. Well, that's what Emma thought, and she used to remind him of that every so often. Emma was also self-confident but was naturally somewhat quieter than Mike. Despite this she easily forged a warm friendship with Richard and Sue. In part, she felt this was helped by their common interests. As a nurse, she often found topics of mutual interest to discuss with Richard. In particular, she derived much benefit from discussing how the medical dynamics had evolved in recent times and how they were continuing to evolve at the current time. At the same time, their mutual interests in swimming also formed an easy topic for discussion. When Emma, Mike and Richard were together, Richard would often teasing Mike about him never quite matching up to his father's prowess from many years before and Emma used to join in with this friendly banter. "Call that a fast time for 100m?" he often used to say, before continuing with "we used to do those times in our warm-up sessions!" These sorts of exchanges were always meant in a good-humoured way. Emma always used to smile when she would see Richard's mock indignation turn into the hint of a smile, closely followed by a quick wink to her, usually as Mike had averted his gaze, just to let her know he was only teasing Mike. It was fair to say, that, over time, maybe a year or so, Richard and Sue became almost 2nd level parental figures to her.

CHAPTER II

7 Years earlier (Emma aged 10)

When Emma was about 10 years old, she remembered an event that had happened in her life that would ultimately change her life forever. It was an otherwise ordinary day. It was a Saturday morning so no school to attend and, like most other Saturdays it signalled a day when she could largely do her own thing: text, and chat online with her friends, listen to music at home and generally chill out at home. She sometimes went out to the nearby local park just to walk or ride her bike. But this Saturday morning was different. Her Dad was out, having visited the local shops to buy a few basic provisions. After eating breakfast with her mom, she felt she could almost sense something was in the air. She was unsure quite what that was but felt that her mom was somewhat ill at ease. It was little surprise therefore when her mom had suggested they should have a little chat. Emma was unsure what to feel or think at this. Her Mom only used the words 'a little chat', when typically, she had something quite important to share. She had used the same words when her mother's elderly aunt had suffered a stroke a year earlier, from which she'd sadly never recovered. On another occasion, she had again used those words before telling her that her father had some challenges at work that might have meant he'd be facing redundancy and lose his job. She recalled at the time that that was the first time she had even heard the word 'redundancy' and didn't really know what it had meant. Her Mom had had to explain that to her at the time. As it was, this was something that eventually blew over for her father and ultimately, the threat of redundancy was lifted.

But this time, it was different. Certainly, Emma's immediate instincts had proven to be correct. Her Mom had just made herself a cup of coffee and sat down next to Emma at the breakfast table.

"Emma", she started. "I want to share something with you. Something about you and me and your dad. There's nothing to worry about at all, but I feel you're old enough to be told." She paused for a moment, as if gathering her thoughts.

"First" she said, "you *know* that we both love you lots, right?" At this, she felt herself nodding in agreement but Emma's level of both interest and concern had suddenly increased. She picked up on the extra accent her mom had used on the word 'know' and suddenly, inside, she registered a certain level of internal alarm inside her. What on earth was her mom about to share with her ... was another family member ill? were they about to split up? To say that what followed was a surprise would certainly have been a huge understatement.

Her mother continued, "before you were born, it hadn't been easy for me to become pregnant". Again, she paused, as if to gather her thoughts, and maybe to summon some additional inner strength to help her continue with what she was saying. "We'd tried for a few years, but I simply didn't get pregnant". "You don't need to know all the details, but there is something I want to share with you. When people like me and your dad have these sort of problems ...". She briefly speeded up here as she then said "and there are *lots* of people like us in a similar situation ... and then there's another route we can use to help us. And we decided to use this other route. We were able to use support to help me get pregnant". Immediately, she picked up on that word 'support'. What on earth did that mean?

"Support, Mom? How do you mean?"

Her Mom went on. "Well, maybe support's not the exact word to use, but, well, we used what's called a donor to help us".

By now Emma was finely tuned in to hearing every single word her mother was telling her. At school within the last year, she'd understood the bare essentials about the birds and the bees and was aware that a new infant was the result of a union between cells from her mom and her dad that then grew into a new baby in her mom's tummy.

Emma immediately continued, "a donor? How does that work, exactly?"

"Well, Emma ... the donor was another man who helped us out".

At this, there was a longer pause from Emma, perhaps because she was still trying to understand what her mother had just shared with her. As much due to sheer ignorance, she was not quite sure what to make of the scenario.

"How did he help out?" she finally uttered.

Her Mom had been dreading this moment for some time, although now she'd finally grasped the nettle, she felt obliged to continue.

"Well, you know to make a new baby, the ... em, cells, have to come from both the mom and dad." She had had a personal fear or dread of having to use the word sperm, as she felt it started to make the tone somewhat more 'sexual' and she remained keen to keep the level of conversation as formal, simple, and factual as she could. She went on "and so, this man ... who was the donor, provided the cells .... that, combined with my, er, cells, to help us make the new baby. You", she added, hoping that it didn't sound like a complete afterthought.

Emma remained quiet for a few seconds longer, before exclaiming with a half quizzical and half indignant tone "So Dad isn't really my dad?"

Her Mom had also been dreading a question like this one, along with a few others so she was somewhat prepared having thought the matter through many times in advance and was quick to respond.

"Of course he is, Emma! He's your dad; he loves you lots – just as I do. We are always here for you, you know that, right? It's just that ... well, *biologically*, - "... she deliberately emphasised the word by saying it more slowly – "the male 'cells' were donated by another man".

"So ... who is he ... this other man?" quizzed Emma.

"Oh, well, we don't actually know who he is, Emma. They don't tell us information like that. Those are part of the rules. They're anonymous donors." She was sincerely hoping this response would satisfy Emma, at least for a while, to allow for a little breathing space. She was sure that she would be mulling over what she'd shared with her.

Emma just said "Ok" in a succinct enough manner to suggest to her mom that, at least for the present, she was 'okay' ... but that she would probably need time to properly make sense of what she'd been told.

"Listen, Emma", her mom went on, "you know we can talk more about this any time you want, okay?"

At this, Emma just nodded briefly. To move on, her mom drank the last remnants from her coffee cup, glanced up at the kitchen clock, before saying "oh, the time's getting on, your dad will be back soon, I'd better get on". And with that, she stood up and made to quickly swill and wash the coffee cup in the sink.

Emma also got up and said, "I'm just ... going to my room for a bit".

"Okay", said her mom. "And don't forget, I'm always here if you want to chat anymore."

Over the next few hours, and indeed over the coming days, Emma thought a great deal about what her mom had told her. Mainly, she was forming more questions in her mind, and she felt herself having an internal dialogue with herself. 'Who was this donor man? Why couldn't the man she knew as her dad all this time have also been her 'biological Dad'? Would she ever get to know who her biological Dad was? Who was he, what was he like, where is he now?' The questions came thick and fast, but, as with most things, her curiosity gave way, with the passing days, such that she was able to re-focus on her general daily living habits. That said, she didn't forget about the topic, and, on a frequent basis, she found herself thinking back to the topic. This was to continue with regularity from that day forwards.

CHAPTER III

2 Years earlier (Emma aged 15)

By the time Emma was 15, her thoughts about her genetic father had moved on considerably. Quite often the thought was put to the back of her mind, and it assumed a presence not unlike that of having a small splinter in a finger. Much of the time she wasn't particularly conscious of the issue, but then when you do have a splinter you can suddenly pick something up and the pressure against the ensuing site of the splinter triggers the respective neurons which in turn signal the pain receptors and the memory is again jolted into recognition. At such times when she did find herself thinking about the topic her mind fired series of random thoughts. Two particularly recurring thoughts were that, first, she could find herself walking past a man in the street one day who could be her biological father and yet both would be blissfully unaware of the biological link they both shared (how totally weird might that be?!) and second, he might simply no longer be alive!

Of course, when Emma was first told, 5 years earlier, it was her 10-year-old brain trying to make sense of what she'd learned. In the ensuing years, although inquisitive, she still remembered some awkwardness of that initial conversation she'd had with her mom and, largely as a result, she'd shied away from discussing the topic further. At the same time, her intellect and cognitive abilities had increased at pace and these, in combination with simple technological advances of the day, meant this had provided her with a spectrum of additional tools and strategies at her disposal to explore the topic further: not least, the internet!

The burning desire to know more about her biological father continued to itch away at her on both subconscious and conscious levels. Sometimes, in a brown study or daydream she might be simply people watching when out and about, observing those around her, seeing other families, parents with children, having fun and going about their daily lives. How many of *them* were also concealing similar secrets? How many other children were walking around, perhaps totally oblivious of the fact that *their* parents might not be the people who had procreated them? Of course, during such quite casual observations, she found herself developing a keen eye for noticing any familial traits that effectively gave away the genetic linkages. Often, it was the somewhat inevitable similarities between the parents' and offspring's heights, general body shape and facial characteristics. At other times, it might be certain facial characteristics and complexion or even their gait. But then, when she happened to notice any obvious inconsistencies, she found herself analysing those habits further. Was she simply over-analysing? Was she also in danger of simply making huge assumptions along the way? Just because two children happened to be walking along with two adults, that didn't automatically mean that they were their parents. They could quite easily be other relatives, or maybe one was their child, and one was the child's school friend. The more she analysed, the more she felt her inner sense of frustration grow. What did it matter about these other people? All these analytical observations did nothing to explain *her* situation.

And so, Emma's quest had begun. Although she didn't quite realise it at the time, she approached the task with the same degree of rigour one might have expected from having to complete an erudite school assignment. Where does one start? Any research begins on a fact-finding mission to gather as much information on the topic to develop a strategy to determine your next steps. Only, with a school assignment, the 'strategy' would have been to assemble your talking points with a view to logically support any hypothesis before going on to draw any conclusions. For Emma, this is where her quest markedly differed. From the outset, she had no idea where this might lead.

Initially, her searches on the internet were challenging; simply entering a search for 'sperm donors' brought up more than a million matches! She quickly realised the scope of the problem for couples encountering problems with infertility. Although these sites were not really what she was looking for, as much out of pure curiosity she found herself clicking on one or two sites for 'donor search'. The level of detail she saw amazed her. Suddenly, the entire process appeared to her to be akin to a mail order service. There were checkboxes for selecting a huge array of physical permutations such as height, ancestry, hair, and eye colour. There were also some more technical sections assessing things such as specimen type. Here, Emma learned how little she really knew about the topic. Although she understood that IVF stood for in vitro fertilisation, she had no idea what some of the other acronyms stood for such as IUI or ICI. She made a mental note to look these up separately. Yet another section sought to address further granular details about potential donors, including, what seemed to Emma at least, criteria that verged on the bizarre. Who on earth would want to consider a donor's astrological birth sign? After all, wasn't that just some false personality humbug for nothing more than pure entertainment with no true scientific basis at all?

Amongst the plethora of different sections and multiple drop-down menus for making your search, there were two sections that particularly caught Emma's eye. These were 'Face Match' and, the very first section at the top of the form, 'Donor Type'. Emma had somewhat naively believed that there was only one 'donor type', but this section had 3 optional checkboxes; 'any'; 'non-ID' or 'ID'. Thankfully, there was a question mark symbol alongside the section to find out more. Emma clicked on the question marks in turn, to discover that this was a crucial piece of information. The 'non-ID' donors agreed to participate as donors but asked *not* to have their identifying information shared with any recipients or adult children. In contrast, any donors checking the 'ID' box *agreed* to allow the sperm donor company to release identifying information on request, **to the registered child once they reached 16**, or older.

These findings sparked further thoughts in Emma, and she felt that she had to learn more. The desire insider her to learn more about her biological father simply kept growing with each newly learned facet of the process that she'd acquired from her initial research. Who was this man who was her biological father? The question now became a repetitive mantra in her head. Then again, she was still just 15. How much more could she possibly find out given that, in the eyes of the law at least, she was still 'just a child'. Almost contradicting what she'd learned, the words her mom had said to her continued to resonate … "we don't actually know who he is. They don't tell us information like that. Those are part of the rules. They're anonymous donors." Consequently, she decided to quiz her mom some more on the topic.

Now she wondered even more. Was her mom simply lying to her? Not in any malicious way or intent to be deceitful, but, if her mom maybe wasn't exactly sure, perhaps this was just her way of attempting to close the topic down so that Emma would maybe accept what she'd said at face value and consider there was nothing more to really learn about her biological father. Mulling over this thought for several days, she decided that she would take one of two options. Either she would simply quiz her mom again and share a few facts from what she'd found on the internet. Or she would continue to research the topic some more and, if she felt brave enough, she would consider phoning one of these companies to find out some more.

Internally, she still felt that it was an awkward topic to bring up again with her mom. First, she had detected some unease on her mom's part when she'd first shared this information with her some years earlier. Partly because of this she'd kept her thoughts largely to herself for fear of worrying her mother with additional enquiries on the matter. If she were to bring it up again, would that signal to her mom that she still wanted to persevere on this topic to find out more? Would it suggest that she was unhappy or maybe anxious about the situation? Worse still, would it indicate that she wanted to take this a long way further forwards in an ultimate quest to try to identify her biological father? In short, would her mom feel that Emma was trying to prize open the casing of a potentially huge can of worms? Weighing up all these facts, Emma decided that she'd continue her internet research and, one day, before too long, she would pluck up the courage to call one of these companies to find out more. Only then, hopefully armed with some useful additional information, would she consider opening a further dialogue with her mom on the topic.

So, which clinic to call and what questions to ask? In total she'd looked at perhaps 3 or 4 sites and in large part they had all been similar in terms of the overall content. These seemed to be the prime thoughts at the front of her mind. The first site she'd found on the internet seemed as good as any. But what questions to ask? Also, she was reticent about calling from her house for fear of anyone else being present. She assumed that it was perhaps not feasible to call at the weekend, thinking that such companies simply might not be open or had limited opening times. She therefore decided to try calling them one lunchtime using her mobile phone. She could find a quiet place on the school campus where she wouldn't be disturbed, and she could talk in a sufficiently relaxed manner. The pre-determined day arrived and, during the morning she found the thought was never far from her mind. So much so that she found her powers of concentration waning during the mornings' lessons. Lunchtime began at noon and, along with her school colleagues this signalled a mass exodus to the school cafeteria. After eating her lunch which, that day, seemed a most uninteresting task, she found herself thinking much more about the ensuing phone call she was to make and her eating was, not surprisingly, somewhat more hurried than normal.

With her meal finished she hurriedly made her way from the canteen. She'd thought ahead as to where she should go to make the call. The sports playing fields were very expansive and, on the far side was a small pavilion used to keep an array of sports equipment, from javelins to shots to high jump bars and footballs. Ahead of her she could see a few small gatherings of friends, 2 or 3 in number. In other places, somewhat larger groups had made a small makeshift football 'field', playing what looked to be a 4-a-side game. It was all very informal. The old 'jumpers for goalposts' cliché sprang to mind, which was a precise description. Over by the pavilion she could see hardly anyone. Indeed, there was no one in sight for some 30 yards or more from the pavilion. She casually walked towards the pavilion and, once there, she sauntered to one side, so she was partially obscured from view. She reached into her pocket and pulled out her phone. In the same pocket was a folded piece of paper on which she'd written the number of the IVF centre. She unfolded the paper and started to tap in the number. After a short delay she heard the phone ringing at the other end. One ring. Two rings. Three rings. Oh no, she thought, don't say they switch the phone off at lunchtimes! She half expected an answerphone message to kick in at this point, but no! Just before the 4th ring, the phone was picked up and Emma heard a female voice "good afternoon, Northeast Cheshire IVF clinic here, Alison speaking, how can I help you?" Although Emma had gone through this moment countless times in her head, the moment still caught her slightly unawares.

"Oh, hi," she said. Almost biding for time a little she went on, "I wonder if you can help me. I'm trying to find out about my father ... my *biological* father. I'm ... well, I have a father and mother who've brought me up, but, well, my mom told me a while ago that my father ... the man who's brought me up, actually isn't my real, well, *biological* father".

As she paused to take a breath, the woman at the other end jumped in:

"Can I just stop you there. Is this an actual enquiry for identifying a past donor?"

"Well, yes" said Emma without thinking too much about the answer. She quickly continued "only my father – my *biological* father, didn't go through your clinic. Well, I don't know which clinic he used. And of course, this was some years ago."

"Listen" said Alison. "I'm the Receptionist here. What I can do is put you through to one of the Research Nurses here who'll be better positioned to address your enquiry. Can you hold a moment?"

"Oh" said Emma. "Er, yes, sure".

The line went quiet momentarily before the silence was broken by some nondescript muzak. Emma wasn't certain but it was some quite calming classical music. 'How very appropriate' she thought, given the sort of people who must phone this clinic. A short while later, certainly less than a minute later, Emma briefly heard Alison's voice again "Emma, just transferring you now to my colleague, Jane ..."

"Hello" said Jane. Emma noticed that Jane's tone sounded calm: she had a very reassuring and confident tone to her voice and Emma guessed that Jane was somewhat older than Alison, the Receptionist. "How can I help you?"

"Oh, well, I was just explaining to your receptionist ..." and Emma effectively repeated, near verbatim, what she'd explained to Alison. Her enthusiasm took hold and Emma felt her pace had quickened. "Oh, yes, it's just that ... I just want to find out ... well ... I'm 17 now and I read on the internet I might have to wait until I'm 18 until ..."

Jane interrupted Emma at this point "Let's not get too far ahead with our thinking at this stage. First things first.

"Right" said Jane. She too, continued "I think I understand your position. Yes, I gathered that might have been the case from what Alison mentioned to me. So, you are 16 currently, is that correct?"

Even if she'd somehow felt the urge to lie, which she didn't, she also relayed what she'd shared with Alison. "Yes, that's nearly right" she said. "I'm 17 right now, my birthday was just a few weeks ago".

"Understood" said Jane. "Well, I'm not sure whether Alison mentioned but, in the first instance, we do encourage people who are making enquiries to visit the clinic in person. We'd strongly urge you to do so in the first instance so we can ensure it's a genuine enquiry and check a few facts and details. As you might imagine, it's a carefully regulated environment. Also, importantly …" Jane paused for a moment before continuing. "You're quite correct in that the rules about the details we hold on file are carefully controlled. You're potentially quite fortunate though as a few things have changed in recent years and it is now possible for us to divulge details to people aged 16 and over now. Tell me, though", Jane continued. "Do you have any details, currently, perhaps from your current family members?"

"No" said Emma. "I know very little. My Mom told me a few years ago that she'd used a donor and it's been on my mind ever since. I did some searching on the internet. That's how I came across your clinic, but otherwise I don't have any other details at all."

"Well, the offer stands, Emma. If you would like to fix up an appointment we could meet up and discuss the matter in more depth."

"Okay", said Emma. "Let me think about it and I can always get back to you, soon." With that, she ended the call. For a moment she just stood there, thinking about the conversation she'd just had. What should she do now? She had no idea really but decided to mull it over for a while. Then, quickly gathering her thoughts she looked around to check her whereabouts again. It was still quiet and there was no one closer than maybe 20-30 yards away. She placed her phone back in her jacket pocket, stepped out from the side of the pavilion and slowly made her way back across the playing fields towards the main school building.

CHAPTER IV

I t was several days later that Emma decided to have a follow up conversation with her mom. Maybe now she was 17 she could get her to open up a little more. She remained convinced that perhaps she knew rather more than she was letting on when they spoke previously. For Emma, the prospect merely created additional anxieties. What would her mom think, now? Would she be concerned that Emma still had more questions and wasn't letting go of the topic? What else DID she know? Was Emma's mind merely working overtime? Despite 5 years passing by, her mom's words from 5 years earlier still resonated strongly in her head "… we don't know who he is, Emma. They don't tell us information like that. Those are part of the rules. They're anonymous donors."

Was that really the complete truth, she wondered?

She finally summoned up the courage to question her mom again. Again, coincidentally, it was a Saturday morning. A bright sunny day. Her father was out, visiting his brother who lived several miles away. Her Mom was busying herself in the kitchen whilst listening to the radio.

Emma sauntered into the kitchen. Her Mom had her back to her as she was waiting for the kettle to boil. "Mom", she said … can I ask you a bit more about my genetic father?"

Immediately, Emma realised that she'd touched that same raw nerve from years ago. Her Mom stiffened slightly and turned round. It's possible that she hadn't even heard her walk into the kitchen, with the sound of the kettle also muffling her entrance so it was perhaps something of a double surprise being startled by her entrance, and her question at the same time. In the time it took her to turn round and catch her gaze, Emma detected that her mom had quickly checked herself. A slight smile appeared across her face and the warm, empathetic voice uttered a motherly response.

"Why, sure", she said. "Was there anything specific on your mind?"

"Well, yes. I mean, I remember what you said before, about you simply not knowing who the donor was, but … I was just wondering if, well, maybe you knew a little bit more but didn't want to share anything me when I asked you before because I was, well … pretty young at the time".

Emma could tell that her mom was listening intently and concentrating intensely on what she was saying. She turned back towards the kettle, which was by now boiling. Emma wondered whether she was taking the opportunity to shield her face … to quickly gather her thoughts to provide an optimal response. What would she say?

"I'm pleased you've come back to me on this" her mom started. Emma thought that maybe she was playing for time, a little. She turned around again to face Emma.

"And, yes, it's true that, of course, you were only 10 at the time when we last spoke about this". She paused a moment before continuing. "You were just a little girl, back then!" Another brief pause and then" … and, of course, we still think of you as our little girl!" This was accompanied by a warm, reassuring smile.

"We do know a little more, Emma and I'm certainly happy to share what we know. It's not much though."

21

"Well?" said Emma, now eager to hear what she had to say.

"Well, as far as we understand it, before donors can become donors, they do have to fulfil certain criteria. I mean they don't just accept anyone off the street, you know!" At this, her face morphed into a slight grin, Emma felt was certainly for reassuring effect.

Her Mom continued "as far as we know he was well-educated; we assume he'd attended University. Although we don't know this for a fact, we gather he may well have been a medical graduate. Apparently, we learned that they often used to use medical grads for this purpose. We're not sure it's that's still the case today – remember Emma this all took place nearly two decades ago. Other than that, we were told a few basic characteristics such as height, weight, hair and eye colour and such like ..." She was about to trail off at this point, but Emma spoke up at hearing this, her level of inquisitiveness suddenly piqued ...

"So, what were you told, then ... about his height and stuff?" she quizzed.

Her Mom again continued. "I'm not sure I can remember all the details. I seem to recall he was around 6 feet tall or so. Otherwise, his weight was average I suppose. Hair and eye colour weren't anything particularly special or unusual, Emma ... brown hair I think, and blue eyes I seem to recall".

"What" said Emma, "and that's it?!" she uttered in an almost incredulous tone.

"Well,", said her mom "there wasn't really much else that concerned us at the time. Our main thoughts were that the sperm donor was essentially someone who'd be, well, relatively fit and healthy. The centre carries out other tests I believe, I think various blood tests and the like, as much to establish that donors don't have any underlying illnesses or health conditions".

Emma was quiet for a few moments, as much taking in and cogitating over this newfound knowledge that had suddenly been presented to her. And then she summoned up an inner courage to pose another question. "And so ... we don't know the donor's name then – or have any way of contacting him?"

Her Mom responded quite abruptly at this question in an almost dismissive way. "No, of course not, Emma. Those details are kept anonymous – as much for the donor's privacy".

"But why?" asked Emma? "I mean, what are they scared of?"

"It's not a question of being scared, Emma. These donors carry out this ... (Emma could detect that her mom was almost struggling for the right word to use at this point) ... service ... out of the goodness of their hearts, to help people like me and your dad. There are lots of people who have these difficulties ... and so we rely on the ... (again, Emma detected her struggling for the right word) ... the ... generosity of these men".

Emma as much felt that the discussion was effectively at an end. She could tell that her mom was starting to erect a bit of a barrier at this point and probably didn't want to be quizzed any more, certainly not at this time, anyway. Emma was mentally sated though, at least for the present as she felt she'd now learned a significant amount of new information about the sperm donor who'd enabled her to be born. However, this new information only served to fuel her continuing interest, and she had already determined that, for her, this research had only just begun. She was determined to dig further.

CHAPTER V

O f course, this topic was also gathering steam at around the same time that her burgeoning relationship with Mike was developing. At first, Emma didn't feel like opening up too much on the topic with Mike, especially given how personal and sensitive it was to her. That said, as their relationship started to blossom, it was something that, little by little, she felt that she wanted to share with Mike.

Having initially broached the topic with Mike he had certainly sounded both interested and supportive, although as the months had passed by, she discerned some wavering in his level of support. It was if he had adopted a position of, well, you've had the benefit of two loving parents who've brought you up, so what further would there be to gain from finding out who your genetic father might be?

Mike also tended to make light of the topic. On one occasion just a few weeks after she'd had the follow up conversation with her mom, they happened to be discussing the topic and, almost in exasperation she'd blurted out to Mike "it's alright for you … you *know* who your mom and Dad are! It's darned obvious looking at the 3 of you …. anyone with one eye could plainly see that you get your general build and long legs from your dad …

along with his general good looks! And let's face it, you and your mom also share the same sense of humour, don't you?

At this, Mike had defended himself with aplomb and neatly turned the tables back on Emma, whilst at the same time attempting to defuse the disagreement and inject some humour … 'Look who's talking?", he said, his intonation rising an octave "why do you think I asked you out in the first place … just take a look in the mirror yourself … and … take a look at *your* long legs …"

Mike's teasing did make her feel good in herself and his tongue-in-cheek comment certainly helped to alleviate the growing tension and caused her to smile a little. However, she felt obliged to have the last word on the topic. "Yes, sure, okay, maybe you've got a point and yes, I admit to having quite long legs, but that's the whole point. Have you seen my mom's and Dad's legs lately?" This was a pointer to the fact that both her mom and Dad were certainly of only average stature, her mom was maybe 5feet 4inches tall compared to her dad who was around 5feet 9inches. Their bodies were in proportion but neither had particularly long legs. With her newfound knowledge gleaned from quizzing her mom she was now totally convinced that her genetic father must have been not only several inches taller than her dad, but she also surmised that perhaps he may have had disproportionately long legs which she'd in turn, inherited from him.

Not to be outdone, Mike in fact ended up having the last comment. He got up from where he'd been sat down and walked across to her. As he got close, he reached out to her hips and pulled her close to him and, with a hint of a cheeky smile on his lips he also allowed his hands to slide down the outside of her thighs and then slowly back up to her waist, "Well listen, I think your legs are just lovely – and that's all that matters. I don't care who you got them from!" He then gave her a quick peck on her lips. Emma had also looped her arms around Mike's shoulders in a warm embrace at this point. As they then released one another, Emma reflected for a moment. While she was prepared to allow this conversation to be closed for the present, she suspected that, otherwise, it would only gravitate into a circular argument if she carried on, so she simply smiled back, half lamely and half sarcastically and kept quiet. She decided though, there and then, that this topic clearly wasn't over. Armed with the facts and information she'd discovered both from the phone call to the fertility clinic and the snippets of additional information from her mom she had every intention of clinging to her quest like a tenacious puppy to find out more about her genetic father.

A few weeks had passed by since she'd had the telephone call to the fertility clinic, and she decided to be brave and reach back out to them to arrange a personal visit as they had recommended. Clearly, she wasn't getting anywhere fast from speaking to her mom … and her conversations with Mike simply weren't geared up in any way to help find out more about her genetic father. He was merely providing some emotional support, although even then she felt that that was becoming somewhat diluted form the last conversation she'd had with him on the topic.

CHAPTER VI

A few days later she called the same clinic and she thought she recognised Alison's voice when she got connected.

"Oh, hello, this is Emma here. I think it might have been you I spoke to a few weeks ago – an enquiry about a past donor". She paused momentarily before continuing with a slightly quizzical tone in her voice …

"I think you put me through to Jane, last time …"

"Hi Emma. This is Alison again and yes; I think I do recall your call from before. Would you like to speak to Jane again, or were you looking to fix up an appointment?"

"Oh", said Emma, "you must have read my mind, there! Yes, Jane had suggested that might be the next best step to take so would that be possible, please?"

"Certainly", said Alison. "Let me just grab the diary … are there any days or times that work best for you?"

"Well, I'm studying A levels now. It's possible I could find an hour or two during the week one day … but are you open at the weekend, at all?"

"Sure", said Alison. "We are open on Saturday mornings when we have a skeleton staff in operation. We work 9-1pm on Saturdays".

"Oh, okay, that'd be great then. Can I fix up to come in on Saturday morning, then, please?"

"We look pretty booked for the next couple of Saturdays. How does 3 weeks' time look for you.? Saturday ... the ... 20th. Would that work for you? Jane's also in that day."

Emma had her small diary to hand. She knew that she could always find time on a Saturday morning. "Yes, that'd be great. What time?"

"How about 10.30am?" said Alison.

"Yes, that's fine, thanks! Are there clear signs where I need to go?"

"Yes", said Alison. "It's the main campus at the Northeast Cheshire Fertility Clinic. Do you have an email, and we can pop the details across to you?"

"Oh, yes", said Emma. She spelled out her email and Alison repeated it back to her for accuracy.

"That's great then, Emma. I'll send the details across to you in the next few minutes. 10.30am on the 20th ... and your appointment will be with Jane who you spoke to before, okay?"

"That's great, thanks so much!"

And, true to her word, less than 30 minutes after the call had ended a new email had popped into her inbox from the fertility clinic. She eagerly opened the email to read the details of the meeting confirmation. Now she just had to be patient for a couple of weeks. She had no way of knowing just how much more she'd find out at the meeting, but she mentally pressed herself to remain positive, at least for the present.

CHAPTER VII

Three weeks later.

It was Saturday 20th. The day of the appointment had finally arrived. The clinic was located some 12 miles away from where she lived so she'd already worked out that she'd have to rely on public transport. She could either have opted for using the bus or the train, but she was looking at needing to use two different bus routes along with a good 1-2 mile walk to reach the clinic. She therefore opted for using the train. There was still around a 10-minute walk to the nearest station from where she lived but, on the map at least, it looked as though the station closest to the clinic was then just a few hundred yards away. She was up bright and early on the Saturday morning and mentioned in passing to her mom that she'd be meeting up with a school friend to grab a coffee in the town and take an hour or two to look around the shops.

Her Mom responded with "Oh, I was going to drive into town later this morning, myself, Emma. Maybe I could give you a lift?"

"No offence, Mom, but this is just a bit of girly time with Rachel from school. Anyway, I'd arranged to meet up with her quite early. I'll be leaving in the next 15minutes or so".

"Oh, okay. Understood" said her mom. She'd uttered the word 'understood', in the certain knowing tone that most middle-aged parents would immediately appreciate: a tone that implied, okay, you're decades younger than me and I totally get that you wouldn't want me around to cramp your style.

Fifteen minutes later, Emma had left the house and was on her way. All the time, in the back of her mind she was thinking, are the next few hours going to completely change my life?

The journey to reach the clinic had, thankfully, been uneventful and she got off the train at the nearby station around 10.15am. Five minutes later she was walking through the main gates of the clinic. She went up to the main entrance, opened the door and walked inside. There was a wide hallway stretching straight ahead and she could see a reception desk window about 10 yards away. She walked towards this window, and she could see a woman seated on the far side who, Emma guessed, was perhaps in her mid-20s.

"Hello" said Emma. The Receptionist had been busy writing something down and, on hearing Emma's voice she looked up and smiled. "I spoke to you a few weeks ago and have an appointment I booked for 10.30am ... my name's Emma".

The Receptionist interjected at this point "Hello, Emma. Yes, we've been expecting you. I'm Alison. Jane's here. Would you just like to take a seat?" – she motioned to a seating area off to one side from the main corridor "and I'll let Jane know you're here".

"Thanks" said Emma, and, with that, she went to take a seat as suggested. It was certainly noticeably quiet and there was hardly anyone else around. She recalled what Alison had said about there being just a skeleton staff on duty on Saturday mornings. She didn't have to wait long. Just a few minutes later a woman appeared from a side door several yards away and walked across to where Emma was seated.

"Hello – is it Emma?' said the woman, "I'm Jane".

Emma was already nodding affirmatively and after briefly saying 'Yes', Jane invited her to follow her to her office.

As they walked towards Jane's office, Jane uttered some general pleasantries and asked Emma if she'd managed to find the clinic okay. "Oh, yes, fine thanks," said Emma. "I came by train, and it was fairly straightforward."

"Oh, that's good". They walked into her office and Jane sat down at her desk, ushering Emma to sit down on one of two chairs on the far side of the desk, opposite her.

"Right" said Jane. "So, I understand you're what we call a donor conceived child and you're after some details about your donor sponsor. As I explained by phone, first we'd like to take some basic details from you and then we can see how best we might be able to help you, okay?"

With that, Jane picked up a pen and opened a folder, taking out two forms. "So, we just need some details about yourself then". Jane spent the next 10 minutes quizzing Emma, apart from her name, address and contact details, she also quizzed her about her current level of knowledge about her donor. Of course, this was challenging for Emma as she was primarily reliant on what her mom had shared with her. That said, in preparation she had also thought a great deal about the topic before arriving and, through working backwards she had been able to extrapolate, to the best of her ability, very approximately when the donor had been 'used'. She felt that her estimate was probably accurate down to 1-3 years either way but around 1998.

After the forms had been completed, Jane spent some time explaining about some of the background processes for locating donors. Emma found this additionally particularly useful, and this included her mentioning that the rules had undergone significant changes in 1991 and again in 2005. Apparently, before 1991, fertility clinics only requested bare minimum information from the donors such as their height, weight and vocation. Since 1991 the rules were changed such that more efforts were made to gather additional information from donors. This included asking donors about their reasons for becoming donors. In addition, donors also had the opportunity to write a personal message to any potential donor recipients. Emma also learned that after 2005, any identifying details about the donor were routinely captured as a matter of routine. It was all starting to sound quite complicated. Jane did end with a summary caveat "of course, there's no guarantee that you will be able to contact the donor. There really are quite a few variables, not only when he became a donor but also what information he might have disclosed at the time. As you can appreciate, from what you've shared your case obviously goes back quite some time and it's not always easy keeping up-to-date records. People move around, relocate even, so it can be tricky. But why don't you leave this with me, and we'll see what we can uncover. No promises I'm afraid but we should be able to get back to you within a week or so with an update".

Emma thanked Jane and left the clinic. Well, she'd taken this big step. She felt what she could only describe as very mixed feelings as she walked back towards the train station. Perhaps she'd have a full identification of her genetic father at last: equally, perhaps it would just be a complete dead end! There was nothing more she could do now but wait to hear back from the clinic.

CHAPTER VIII

F or the next week she did her best to focus on her schoolwork. This, together with her swimming club activities, at least helped to keep her mentally and physically occupied. Every day she still felt her mind wandering back to the topic at any free moment.

Several days had passed by and it was the Friday following her visit to the clinic. She had just had her lunch and was spending a few minutes walking on the school playing fields, coincidentally, she wasn't far from where she'd made that initial call to the fertility clinic just a few weeks earlier, when she heard her mobile phone ring. She quickly removed it from her pocket and answered the call.

"Hello" said the female voice on the line, "is this Emma Bridges?"

"Yes" said Emma, quickly recognising the voice being Jane's from the fertility clinic.

"Hi" said Jane, "sorry it's taken a while to get back to you, but we have carried out our searches and I do have an update for you".

"Oh, that's good news!" said Emma quite excitedly.

"Well, yes" said Jane, "but it's, well, a partial result, really".

"Oh" said Emma, "how do you mean?"

"Well, we have your donor's name on record, but it appears that, well, let's just call it the 'anonymity box' was checked. While that might sound somewhat discouraging, that essentially means we aren't at liberty to disclose his name although we do have some contact details in the form of a telephone number, email and address. And we can also at least confirm that he was a medical student at the time".

"Oh, that's good then, Jane, I suppose?" she ended quizzically.

"In a way, yes", said Jane, "but please remember, some of these details may not be completely up-to-date. But at least you potentially have something to go on here. This scenario does sometimes happen. Donors simply may not wish to have their full identity revealed but, at the same time, they may not mind at least making themselves available should any donor conceived individuals want to contact them to ask any questions such as details about things like their physical characteristics and any other health-related aspects. Some health conditions for example can have a genetic angle so it can prove useful. Do you have a pen, handy? Naturally, I can put what we've found in an email to you and follow up with a formal letter as well, but I guessed you might be keen to have these details now. The email might not get sent out until next week now."

"Absolutely" said Emma. "Hang on just a second". And with that she started rummaging around in her bag. She found a pen and a pencil at the bottom of her bag, and she always carried her small pocket diary with her, so she pulled that out and turned to the section at the back of her diary where there are typically a few blank pages for collecting random notes. Selecting the pen she said, "Okay, go on".

"Right, so here's the address we have:

Flat 3b, New Albert Street, Edinburgh. Sorry but we don't appear to have a post code. The phone number is

0131 532 7967. And finally, the email we have is raw@gmail.com"

"Was that roar as in 'R... O... A... R' or 'raw' as in R.. A.. W..?" asked Emma.

"The latter, Emma," said Jane. "R..A.. W."

"That sounds a bit strange!"

"Well, yes" said Jane "but if you think about it, folks have a lot of leeway around determining their email addresses these days, don't they? It could just be their initials … or a nickname perhaps. Who knows?!"

"Okay" said Emma.

"Well, that's about it, Emma. I hope you find this useful. As I said, I'll put all this down in an email and follow up with a letter, too, okay? Good luck!"

Emma thanked Jane and ended the call. Wow! She thought. Her research could now continue with a fair bit of additional sleuthing now to do. Her mind was full of so many competing thoughts. Edinburgh! A flat! A medical student. So maybe he's a doctor now? And maybe Edinburgh was where he studied medicine? He must have been intelligent, then, she thought. She realised she might well be jumping to conclusions too quickly, so she took a deep breath and started to rein in her thoughts. Still, she felt enthused and quite excited by this newfound information. She was hardly aware of the train journey back home; such was her mind constantly thinking about what she might do next.

She spent much time mulling over the details she'd obtained. First, she decided that she'd continue her sleuthing by herself, at least for the present. Her Mom clearly didn't seem too keen to discuss the topic in any detail and Mike, whilst on one level was being supportive, clearly didn't possess the same level of interest as herself. No, she would take this to the next level herself. Over that weekend she formulated her plan of attack!

Emma was certainly fascinated with the information she'd been given. Edinburgh … and he was a medical student! I wonder where he is right now and what he's doing, she pondered. Maybe an eminent surgeon, perhaps. Would he be married … have a family, living in some prestigious house in an affluent part of the country? The permutations were, quite literally, endless.

She was certainly not thinking that the address would be indicative of where he'd be based currently, supposing that he'd lived there whilst studying, presumably at Edinburgh University. Again, she quickly realised that she was jumping to conclusions here. Her first thought then, was to try the phone number – 0131 532 7967. Emma had once or twice dabbled on the internet looking to track phone numbers in the past, but she'd concluded that that was quite a hit and miss affair at the best of times. She spent a few minutes searching around for any clues but quickly realised that it was proving fruitless. There was nothing else for it, she'd simply have to call the number. It was the Monday after she'd visited the clinic. Again, she was at school, and it was her lunch break. This had become the general time when she could grab time for herself to make such calls. She pressed in the numbers and listened intently. After several rings it was answered. A male voice at the other end, with a marked Scottish accent said "Hello?"

Emma began to talk. "Oh, hello … I wonder if you can help me. I'm trying to track someone down and this is the last number I've been given for him".

"This is the number of a private residence. Who is it you're looking for?" said the Scottish voice.

Emma continued, "Well, that's where it gets a bit tricky. I don't actually have a name, as such, but the one thing I do know is that he was a medical student and it's possible he was studying at Edinburgh University, quite a few years ago in fact".

"You're trying to track someone down and you don't have a name?" the voice at the other end quizzed with an incredulous tone to his voice.

Emma had thought as to how the conversation might play out, should she be successful enough to get to speak to someone and, similarly, she too thought it might come across as somewhat strange, trying to find someone whose name you don't even know. Consequently, she'd decided that honesty would be the best policy and she'd be prepared to explain the background in sufficient detail to allow an understanding of her predicament.

She continued: "Oh, I should maybe have explained ... the person I'm looking for would have been up in Edinburgh about 20 years ago ...". She was steeling herself at this point, about to disclose more background about her quest to find her biological father, but the man on the other end had already interjected at this point.

"20 years ago?!" he said, with a definite sense of exasperation in his voice. "Sorry love, I don't think I can help you, even if you did have a name. I'm a landlord here but I've only been here for around 8 years and I'm quite sure the property changed hands a few times before me over the previous 20 years or so. It's been used as student digs for a quite a while, but I wouldn't have a clue about past students, certainly not from that long ago. You'd probably be on a wild goose chase trying to track down past landlords".

Emma was crestfallen." Oh, okay. I understand. Thanks. Sorry for troubling you."

"Aye, nae problem" were the final words from the other end. And she then ended the call.

Emma was generally a glass half full type of girl, so although this was not the news she'd been hoping to hear, at the same time, it was something she was now able to tick off. If anything, it certainly added weight to the idea that he'd been a medical student at Edinburgh, and this was where he'd been living during that time. She had no guarantees of this, but she felt it was a reasonable assumption for her to make. Oh well, thought Emma, one door closes …

She still had this rather unusual email. Of course, this too might not prove especially useful. Maybe it was no longer valid. She decided there was only one way to find out and, later that same day she started crafting the email to send to 'raw@gmail.com'. But what to say?

Initially tempted to explain the full background she erred instead, on a very brief content, her aim to be to establish that the email was still valid. She felt she could always elaborate further as necessary, when, or just as likely, if she should get a response. At the same time, she recalled what Jane had mentioned when they'd met … '***the anonymity box had been checked***'. So, it was clear that he didn't want to be formally identified or named. But then, Emma thought, this was from some 20 years ago. Would the donor still be feeling the same way, especially once he was to realise that Emma was the outcome of his donor efforts? Would that scare him off? Would he be curious? Would he be pleased … and maybe want to meet up? So many questions, thought Emma. She felt she was getting closer to finding some real answers, but equally, there was nothing properly tangible for her to grasp onto.

Crafting the email took longer than she had anticipated. She started scribing too much, in her estimation, then deleted parts and re-typed. She did this several times until it started to become a little frustrating. In the end, she decided on the following verbiage:

25th April
From: emmab@gmail.com

General enquiry
To: raw@gmail.com
Hello,

You don't know me, and we haven't met before but I'm trying to track down an old family friend from some years ago, more than 20 years ago in fact. I was given an Edinburgh address and phone number which haven't proved fruitful. I was also given this email and I'm led to believe the person was a medical student in the past. Are you able to help me please?

Emma

She clicked 'send'. She could do no more. It was sent. Either he would reply, or he wouldn't. And if he didn't, she'd simply have to accept that and maybe that might even close the door entirely on her quest. She accepted she would just have to wait and see.

To say that Emma was surprised when an email response appeared in her inbox less than 2 days later, would certainly be an understatement. Immediately, she could see it was from 'raw'. This could be it, she thought, the moment she would finally make proper contact with her genetic father ...

Eagerly, she opened the email.

27th April
From: raw@gmail.com
To: emmab@gmail.com
Hello Emma,

Thanks for your note. Can you divulge where you obtained my email from, please?

Thanks ...

Emma was left somewhat dumbfounded by the brief content. Clearly, she'd found a live email account with someone at the other end. Was this her genetic father?

She still didn't have that confirmed. And how very brief the content, not signing off with his name even. She felt this was almost verging on the brusque, as if he didn't really want to be contacted.

She quickly decided to respond and felt she would err on the side of transparency. After all, if this was her genetic father, she desperately wanted to make some sort of contact. She'd only be divulging the truth … just facts, really.

27th April
From: emmab@gmail.com
To: raw@gmail.com
Hello again,

Thanks for replying. To put you a bit more in the picture, I'm trying to trace my genetic father. I gather this might be you. I obtained your contact details from the Northeast Cheshire Fertility Clinic recently. Are you able to confirm that I'm contacting the correct person?

Warm regards,

Emma

Well, this would be it, she thought. Either he'd respond back promptly, or maybe he'd be totally freaked out and wouldn't respond at all.

This time, however, the response came back even more promptly … the next day in fact. Again, she quickly opened the email:

28th April
From: raw@gmail.com
To: emmab@gmail.com
Hello Emma,

Thanks for clarifying your situation. To confirm, yes, it would appear I am your genetic father. I was a donor quite a while ago. I thought my details would be retained anonymously though. I certainly wasn't anticipating being contacted like this out of the blue. Did you have any specific questions for me?

Regs …

Progress, thought Emma! At last, confirmation it was him. She'd found him. That said, she still felt somewhat bemused by the email content. It was great to get the confirmation, but, well, he made it all sound very matter of fact. Emotionless almost. He certainly didn't sound particularly happy about the situation. And he still hadn't signed off with his actual name! She found this all a bit impersonal and, innocently, she was secretly hoping for more. A sense of inquisitiveness from him if nothing else.

Again, she quickly responded but this time she felt she'd ask a few more direct questions.

28th April
From: emmab@gmail.com
To: raw@gmail.com
Hello again,

Thanks once more for replying and confirming that you are, in fact, my biological father. It's something of a relief to have finally found you. I'm sorry if you feel it's a bit of an imposition me contacting you in this way but I was only going on the information that the clinic was allowed to provide to me now I'm 17 years old. I don't wish to cause you any anxiety at all and I'm simply curious to learn a bit more about you if possible. I'm not even sure of your name or where you're based. I believe the clinic mentioned that you may have been a medical student at the time. I live in Kendal in Cumbria. Are you able to share any more details please? Depending on where you're located would it be possible to arrange a brief meeting?

Warm regards,
Emma

Emma now felt as if she were being about as direct as she could be and, when several days passed by, she genuinely thought that she'd stepped over the mark and 'raw' had simply had enough and was not going to respond any more. The days lapsed by. A week had passed, and it was now the first week of a new month. And still nothing. One week became 2 weeks. She'd blown it! She was convinced. After 2 weeks she wondered whether to just send him a friendly reminder email, but the decided against doing so.

CHAPTER IX

I t was on the 15th day that she received another email.

13th May
From: raw@gmail.com
To: emmab@gmail.com
Hello Emma,

Apologies for the delayed response but work has been terribly busy of late. I'd be okay with meeting up with you, although I don't really have any wish for this to become a regular occurrence. But more of a 'one off' visit would be acceptable to me. Would you be comfortable with this arrangement?

Can I just check. Apart from you and me ... and the Clinic of course, does anyone else know about this?

I too am based in the Northwest and not that far from where you're located so it would probably be convenient to meet up.

Nick

Finally!!! Thought Emma. Finally, she would get the opportunity to meet and see her biological father face to face for the first time in her life. It was really going to happen! And, she now had his first name. Nick. She wondered if that was short for Nicholas. But that was a purely trivial thought. She was so happy. Again, although she didn't want to appear particularly desperate in any way, again, she quickly replied to his email.

13th May
From: emmab@gmail.com
To: raw@gmail.com
Dear Nick,

Thank you so much for your latest reply. It's wonderful to hear you'd be amenable to meet up and I totally understand when you say about not wanting this to become a regular occurrence. I'd be fine with that. (Although inside, Emma felt quite disappointed to hear him say this, she didn't want that disappointment to be conveyed in the words of her email. Secretly, she felt that, if she could get to meet him, he'd be so impressed to see what a sparkling young lady she'd become that he'd maybe decide to change his mind and want to see her again. Then again, was this just her naivety running riot in her mind?)

How about meeting up for coffee one Saturday morning perhaps? Please let me know if that would work for you.

Warm regards,

Emma

Ps And no, it's just you and me who know about this.

She clicked send.

CHAPTER X

25ᵗʰ April in Richard White's home study

I t was the early evening. Richard was juggling his time between checking his emails – mainly to and from other clinicians and a variety of medical practices, ethics committees and the like along with the ubiquitous email approaches made, in large part, by sales reps - and boning up on the latest medical literature. He had online access to both the British Medical Journal (aka the BMJ) and The Lancet and, for many years these had formed the mainstay of his efforts to maintain as up to date as possible on the latest research findings. It was a never ending and largely thankless task but, as a longstanding GP he'd grown accustomed to this practice that had been forged since he'd started off in medical practice.

His email account indicated receipt of yet another email. He glanced at his inbox. Unusually, the title header simply indicated 'General enquiry' and he could see straightaway that it was not one of the usual contacts with whom he had regular contact. Largely because of this and with his curiosity piqued he went immediately to open it. It was the email sent by Emma Bridges, but from the sender's email line it merely indicated 'Emmab' ... The content shocked him into laser mental focus. It took him a few moments to grasp the topic. 'An old family friend?' ... 'Edinburgh' ... 'medical student'. Who exactly was this person? Whoever it is, she appears to already know a few things about me, he thought. Certainly, he had been based up in Edinburgh during his medical undergraduate days, so those facts added up. 'An old family friend'? The words kept whirling around in his head. He certainly couldn't think of any old family friends who might fit into this bracket.

The nature of his work meant that he had developed an air of healthy cynicism where emails were concerned. These days you often had to tread carefully given all the scammers and fraudulent emails that did the rounds. This was one reason he'd created a cryptic email that didn't divulge either his first or second name in the title, but instead drew quite simply on his initials. By a quirk of fate, his middle name of Alan, enabled him to spell our 'raw'. He'd often mused as to whether his parents had cottoned on to this fact before choosing his first and middle names. It was something that he had never got to the bottom of, although with the passing years it seemed to become less important and more trivial. But that said, this email he'd just received was ... different. Richard felt that it could be genuine. Nevertheless, he didn't jump to respond, although it did play on his mind for the next day or two and so, a couple of days later he decided to respond. He decided to keep it brief and 'play along' as much to see where it was going. He crafted his one-line reply to try and uncover more from 'Emmab'. In addition, he deliberately and very cautiously omitted from signing off with his name at the end of the email.

He was shocked to see the speed of response from Emmab. Barely 15 minutes had passed since he'd sent his response before he received Emmab's reply. And the content then started to send shock waves through him. If she was to be believed, and currently, he had no strong compulsion to disbelieve her, this girl/lady was quite possibly his biological daughter!!! The other factors added up. Back in his undergraduate days, along with several of his peer group, they had decided to volunteer to be sperm donors. He remembered clearly one of his lecturers casually remarking about the opportunity. "It's an easy and, ahem, quite a pleasurable way for you to supplement your medical tuition fees" he'd said, before continuing ... "it'll certainly pay some of your beer money ... and, of course (and Richard had felt he said the next piece as something he was obliged to say) ... you will potentially be providing much needed support to many of those would be parents out there who otherwise might never realise that aspiration of becoming parents". Okay, he'd thought at the time. This was win: win! It wouldn't take much of his time to produce a few samples: he'd be doing his bit for the wider community from a fertility perspective needs AND he'd get some cash in his pocket for the privilege. What wasn't to like? He had gladly volunteered at the time, as had quite a number of his medical undergraduate colleagues. He *thought* he'd checked an anonymity box at the time so that he wouldn't ever experience the situation he was currently facing. This was another reason for him wanting to check out this 'Emmab', if indeed, Emma was in fact her name. How could he know that for sure? And was the 'b' the initial letter of her surname? Again, he realised he was guessing. Suddenly, for no apparent reason the name Emma Bunton came into his head. Surely it wouldn't transpire that one of the Spice Girls was his genetic daughter!! Bizarre as that sounded, he suddenly found himself, quite irrationally, almost in autopilot mode quickly opening a search engine and typing in her name. It was with some sense of relief when he saw that she was in her early 40s and he couldn't help but chuckle to himself at the fearsome thought that he'd allowed to enter his mind just a few moments earlier.

Richard didn't have any other underlying suspicion at this stage of anything potentially nefarious from this email exchange and so he decided to play along a little further. If it was genuine, he was now interested to learn what she was after. He responded back to her, opening a little more but still omitting to include his name at the end.

Just as with the previous email he'd sent, it was almost as if 'Emmab' was hovering over her email account 24/7 and a further reply arrived within 30 minutes. Only this time, the content included two items of information that now triggered hugely worrisome thoughts in his head: she had now divulged that she was 17 years old and lived in Kendal. Now another distinct ... and eminently more likely but at the same time bizarre coincidence had entered his mind. Emma B could be Emma Bridges: his son's steady girlfriend! Certainly, her first name, age and location ticked all the boxes!

Richard White was a very experienced General Practitioner. The years of medical training along with the many years of acting in this capacity had taught him early on to remain calm, especially in the face of adversity. It's others who panic, not doctors! Doctors remain calm and deal with problems, often incredibly effectively. This same dynamic immediately kicked in after reading Emma's latest email.

Richard was not only highly intelligent, but he had also moved with the times and had taught himself to become technologically savvy. This was largely borne out through a couple of past unfortunate incidents involving the odd altercation with one or two angry patients. Seemingly quite minor at the time, he had quickly learned that it was one thing to have the odd disagreement with a patient perhaps about a clinical diagnosis or opinion. It was quite another thing for such patients to decide to gravitate to social media to drum up a storm against him. Thankfully, he had used his charm, guile, and ultimately conciliatory manner to defuse such situations when they had occurred, but it had taught him some useful lessons. Not least of these were a few technical tips and tricks he'd acquired for establishing additional information about individuals who may have sent emails to him. He knew, for example a few ploys for extracting additional identifying features about the sender such as quickly identifying their IP address. In addition, he was also aware of internet sites for tracking such details and identifying linkages. Within minutes of receiving the latest response from Emmab it was this ploy he quickly used and, within 15 minutes of receiving Emma's last email he had quickly found a variety of linkages that included one reference to the local swimming club and another that included a group image showing several club members in a team photo: his worst fears were confirmed. It was definitely her!

Just as his medical training had equipped him to robustly deal with medical crises, similarly, although his nerves were jangling at this point, it was as if his brain had shifted up a couple of gears to draw on reserve powers of creative inspiration to fathom out what course of action to take next. He paused at his keyboard and looked up. He could see out of his study window into his garden and the view beyond that showed some distant fields and hills in the distance. After a few seconds of inactivity where he found himself in an almost daydream state, his focus returned to his computer and then, a moment later up to an adjacent wall, on which was a framed document. Although it was too far away to be able to properly read the text the top two lines were legible, just, in red font. 'Bachelor of Medicine' and 'Bachelor of Surgery' beneath it. For a moment he was transported back to his medical undergraduate days and images came into his head from that time. He clearly remembered the moment when he had graduated and, three Latin words sprang to mind, *'primum non nocere'.* Popularly attributed to the Hippocratic Oath, the English translation equates to 'first, do no harm'.

And now, here he was, facing frankly a quite bizarre situation where he needed to decide what best course of action to take. This wasn't a medical dilemma, as such, but it was a dilemma all the same. His analytical mind was considering multiple facets, back and forth, repeatedly. He didn't really want this to go *anywhere*. He'd prefer to nip it in the bud and put a swift end to the matter. While it wasn't anybody's fault (or was it (?) ... he still felt the Fertility Clinic may have shown some dereliction of duty around privacy laws, although he couldn't be certain and would have to check on this ... And what about Emma ... her feelings? What about Mike and his feelings (should *he* ever find out?) Similarly, what of his wife, Sue? Emma's parents, Linda, and James? Did any of them already have any inkling? By any stretch of the imagination, it was a messy scenario, and it required a cool head and an equally calm and logical assessment to determine the optimal next steps to take.

There was a lot to consider, and various ideas were spinning around his head. His training had taught him many times in the past to sleep on things wherever possible to do so, before making any knee jerk reactions. One plan started to take definite shape in the ensuing days, but he decided to mull it over a while before deciding his next steps.

About a week later, his plan was decided. First, he felt it would be best to try to bring things to a head by arranging a meeting with Emma, although he certainly had no intention whatsoever of meeting her himself! No, his plan would include calling on a big favour from an old friend. Ultimately, he wanted to provide an opportunity for Emma to have her meeting and to ask any questions she may have, but then to quickly end the association. He also had the awkward problem of seeking to find a way of ending her relationship with Mike in as painless a way as possible. He still hadn't thought of the best way to go about doing that.

On 8th May, Richard found himself on LinkedIn and sifting through his myriad connections. Scrolling through them he came to the one he'd been looking for – Terry Parker. He'd been connected to Terry for a few decades. They'd met at Edinburgh University when they were both studying medicine and, in a short time, had become firm friends. They'd kept in touch ever since and, by chance had both ended up as GPs living and working in the North of England. Terry lived some 30 miles away from Kendal in the Yorkshire dales, operating as a local village GP. They typically met up at least once or twice a year, typically to go for a hike in the fells and grab a drink and a pub lunch to catch up and reminisce a little. They had both supported one another over the years and were committed friends. Richard sent a message across via LinkedIn: 'Terry, it's been a while, we should catch up. Are you around this week at all? I have something I need to run by you., Best, Richard'.

Terry typically responded quickly, assuming he wasn't on vacation and, sure enough just a day later he'd replied.

'Richard, Great to hear from you. Are you around this afternoon? Let's chat'.

Richard immediately responded back.

'That's great Terry. I can call you at 2.30pm. Hope that works for you.'

Within minutes, Terry had responded back with a simple winking emoji icon.

At 2.30pm on the dot, he called Terry's number. He picked up at the 3rd ring.

"Terry Parker here?"

"Terry!" said Richard," how the devil are you, my friend?"

"Oh, not so bad, Richard. A few more aches and pains but still the same. And you?"

"Yes, fine thanks. Thanks for agreeing to talk. I don't have long so I'll cut to the chase. There's a ... situation that's arisen and I really need to ask you a big favour."

"Oh" said Terry, "sounds intriguing, old boy. Tell me more. I'm all ears". Terry had a generally jovial nature and Richard realised that what he had to tell him would probably come as quite a shock. Not only that, but the favour would also be the double whammy.

"So, remember when we were at Edinburgh Uni?"

"Won't forget those great times in a hurry!" said Terry.

"Remember back in our 2nd year and we became sperm donors?"

"I certainly do – ha ha!" The chuckle was a thinly veiled attempt to conceal the smugness they'd both felt realising such a pleasurable way of not only spending their time but also in getting financial recompense for the privilege.

"Well,", said Richard. "It's just come back to bite me in the bum ... with very big teeth!"

"How do you mean?", quizzed Terry.

"Well, it appears that a girl that was produced through IVF, using my sperm, has managed to track me down as her biological father!"

There was a moment's pause at the other end before Terry exclaimed "You have got to be kidding me!!" Another slightly longer pause before he continued. "But hang on, we signed that disclaimer, didn't we, to maintain confidentiality, didn't we?!"

"That's exactly what I thought, too," said Richard. "I'm not certain whether there might have been some cock up with the paperwork and/or there may also have been some change in the legal rights for the offspring in these

IVF cases, but, long story kept very short, she's tracked me down and I'm virtually 100% sure it's correct".

Richard could hear Terry take in a deep breath before being about to speak again, but Richard quickly jumped in again.

"And Terry, I haven't told you the worst part ... I'm fairly sure this girl is Mike's steady girlfriend!"

"What?!" said Terry. "Surely not! I mean, how the heck can that even happen?!"

"I know. It's knocked me for six, I can tell you!"

"Are you sure about this. How did you find this out ... and what the heck are you going to do? Have you explained to Mike?"

"Whoa, Terry, hold on mate, what is this, 20 questions! Listen, yes, I'm maybe 99% certain. We've exchanged a few emails – I've got her name, well her first name, assuming it's authentic and I'm quite sure her surname initial, too. I've been careful not to reveal my name yet – although I let slip a bogus first name in the last email I sent. Anyway, in the last email she sent to me she happened to mention her age and the fact that she'd based in Kendal. I quickly did some sleuthing and I've narrowed it down. Trust me, Terry, it's definitely her!" He paused for a breath before continuing.

"You asked what I'm planning on doing. I've thought about this long and hard. Here's my plan. I've suggested a meet up, although I've left her in little doubt that this should just be a one-off meeting and not the start of any regular liaison. Terry, honestly, I'd rather not be having any connection with her at all ... but, like I said, I have a plan, and this is where you come in".

"Me? I'm intrigued, Richard. Tell me more," said Terry.

"So, in my last email I signed off as 'Nick'."

"Nick?!" interjected Terry.

"Yes ... listen, just hear me out ... this is where the favour comes in. I'd like you to meet up with Emma."

"Me?! How the heck does that work?"

"Listen. All she knows so far is my email address – raw@gmail.com and this fictional first name I've divulged as Nick". She has no idea of my identity, just as she has absolutely no idea of your identity. I mean, she doesn't know that 'raw' stands for my initials. I've already thought up a white lie there ... Nick Rawlings."

"What?" said Terry, again interjecting.

"Yes, 'raw' can just be the first few characters of my surname – that's also fictional. All I need is for you to meet up with Emma posing as this fictional character, Nick Rawlings. I can arrange everything else. The meeting, a few things for you to chat to her about. Remember, I've already stressed for this to be a one off and she's bought into this. We can keep the meeting short. I've already got the plan in place."

He could tell that Terry wasn't yet sold on the idea. "Now look Richard, is this going to work? I mean, what if she starts asking some awkward questions – say about where you live and stuff?"

"Like I said" continued Richard. "Already got that covered. Come on, this can just be 30 minutes out of your life to do an old pal a favour ... I'll coach you and take care of all the details. It'll be a cinch. Surely a conversation with a 17-year-old girl isn't going to phase you? I mean what are you, man, or mouse? It's a one-off meeting, that's all. What do you say?"

Terry was tempted to ask for some breathing space to think it over, but he knew that if he did, he'd only start coming up with reasons for not going through with Richard's plan. And Richard was one of his oldest and trusted friends. And if it was just a one-off 30-minute meeting, then surely, he was up to *that*! 'Man, or mouse'.

The words resonated in his head. He'd heard Richard use the expression many times over the years. He recalled him uttering the expression right back in their medical undergraduate days. If they'd had some particularly challenging assignment to carry out, or the first time they were called upon to conduct a new medical procedure, Richard had always been the first one to grasp the nettle and had often used the expression. And he was often right!

Terry continued ... "but what if it gets awkward ... and she wants to continue meeting?"

"Look, I told you, Terry, I've got all bases covered." He threw the curveball straight back at Terry. "How old are we?"

"What?" said Terry. "You know how old we are. We're both in our late 50s!"

"Yes," said Richard. "So, one part of your spiel will be to say you're preparing for early retirement and in a few months' time you're looking to relocate to the seaside. That should sort out that line of questioning. We'll just make out you'll soon be moving hundreds of miles away".

"Remember" said Richard, and he stressed the next words slowly for maximum effect – "She knows absolutely *nothing* about you".

"But ... well, we don't even look alike. I mean, won't she smell a rat?"

"Look. Agreed you don't look that alike but think about it. We're both similar heights, right? I'm 6-foot 1 inch. How tall are you?" It was intonated as a rhetorical question and he simply continued, not waiting for Terry to respond. "And we both have roughly similar colouring. That should be more than enough. I doubt she's going to want to start examining you with a magnifying glass or take a swab from you for a DNA test!"

Terry realised he was gradually being drawn in to accepting the challenge.

"Well, I guess, if it's just a one-off …" he trailed off. "But don't you feel … well, it's wrong to perpetuate the lie?"

"I've already thought about that, Terry. It's her feelings I'm most trying to ameliorate here. Consider the alternative for the moment? The truth." Richard continued but adopted a somewhat mocking tone "Oh hi Emma … did I tell you, by the way, I'm your genetic father? … Yes, so Mike's your half sibling! The poor girl would be devastated. We can spare her any of that heartache."

"Granted", said Terry. "But that still doesn't tackle the problem of her relationship with Mike though, does it?"

"Agreed" said Richard. "But then, it is the first semi-real relationship for the pair of them. I mean, they're still young. Who knows, it's possible the relationship could fizzle out naturally, but maybe I can start to subtly sow some seeds of doubt in Mike's mind. I know they're seeing less of one another since Mike's been at Uni. I could maybe work on that angle. Either way, we both know that that relationship basically can't go anywhere now, for obvious reasons. I'll be honest with you, I do see that as the trickier aspect to tackle, but first things first. Are you okay with this meeting going ahead? Come on, you're not going to let me down, are you? Yes, or no?"

Terry now felt sufficiently sucked in. "Yes. Go on then. But we need to check everything".

"Great" said Richard. "How does next Saturday morning, grab you?"

"Blimey, you don't let the grass grow, do you?"

"Well, look. nothing's firmed up, but, you know, no time like the present. Grasp the nettle and all that, and in her last email she'd suggested catching up for coffee on a Saturday morning. Let's say next Saturday or the one after. Okay? God I really feel like I'm spoiling you, now".

"Let's shoot for the one after then, Richard. I feel I'll still need to get my head around this."

"You'll be fine! I'll suggest Sat the 29th then in my reply to her last email. I'll keep you posted. It'll be a cinch. Trust me! Speak soon, my friend." And with that, he hung up. Richard sat back in his chair, somewhat relieved that the first step in his master plan was about to come to fruition. Once that meeting was able to take place that was one major hurdle overcome in his mind. Inwardly, he realised that Emma and Mike's relationship was still a thorny issue, but, as he said to himself, one step at a time.

CHAPTER XI

He lost no time in getting things started, immediately crafting an email response to Emma.

Sat 15th May
From: raw@gmail.com
To: emmab@gmail.com
Hello Emma,

Thanks again for your last email. Sure, we could meet up for coffee. I'm busy next Saturday so how about the next one – 29th May - would that work for you? It's perhaps easier for me to travel over to you. There's a Costa in Kendal town centre. Presumably, you know where it is. Shall we meet there? If so, let's say 10.30am. I do have other appointments as well that day so could only spare about 30 or 40mins. I hope that's okay.

Let me know.
Thanks,
Nick

As before, Emma was quick to respond. Just a couple of hours later, her reply popped into Richard's inbox.

Sat 15th May
To: emmab@gmail.com

From: raw@gmail.com

Hi Nick,

Thanks – yes, this will work fine for me. 10.30am on 29th May. I very much look forward to meeting up! Btw, here's my mobile number should anything crop up beforehand – 07751 690470.

Warm regards,

Emma

On receipt of Emma's email, Richard quickly picked up the phone and dialled Terry's number. Terry answered.

"Terry Parker here."

"Terry – it's Richard again. Just wanted to let you know. We're 'on' for a meeting on 29th May. I've arranged the meeting at 10.30 on Sat 29th May at the Costa coffee shop here in Kendal. You okay with that?"

"Hi Richard. I guess so. I haven't got any other conflicts that morning and I can drive over okay. How long should we meet for?"

"I've already got that covered, Terry. In my email to Emma, I said I had other appointments so could only chat with her for half an hour or so. You see ... always thinking of you, aren't I? 30 minutes. That'll be a cinch, eh?" Richard didn't wait for Terry to respond but went on – "Listen, I managed to find an image of Emma from one of her recent swimming galas taken a few months ago. I can scan it and send it across to you, so you've got an idea of her appearance. There's not a great deal more to share with you. Remember, the plan is you're effectively posing as one Nick Rawlings ... which will also get us around the origin of my, sorry, 'your' email 'raw@gmail.com'. That'll probably consume 5 minutes of chat when you meet her. Other than that, you know she's doing her A levels and is thinking of going into nursing. She's also a keen swimmer. She's been going steady with Mike for a year or two now. But I guess she'll probably share some of this with you when you meet. Remember, the main thing to get across is just reinforcing that you'll soon be retiring and relocating to the South Coast. You can think up somewhere – maybe Bournemouth. Otherwise, just play along and let the conversation flow. You can be pleasant enough but maybe keep it fairly business like. The intention is for it to be a one-off meeting. And she's already bought into that idea. She believes you're her biological father so you can be a bit empathetic. But don't lay it on too think. You don't need to give much else away. Like I said, it'll be a cinch, mate. Okay?"

"I guess so, Richard. Though it still makes me feel ... he paused ... uneasy. I'm not keen on the fact that we'll be lying to her".

"I hear you, Terry, but look, it's for the greater good. You know the score. Tell you what, on 29th why don't you drop in here first, on your way over? I have a nice drop of single malt in my study if you fancy a little Dutch courage before you meet up with her."

He could hear Terry begin to chuckle at the other end "You don't miss a trick Richard, do you?"

"Come on", said Richard, "we're old mates and I sincerely appreciate what you're doing for me here. It's the least I can do. So, pop by at my place around 9.30am that morning, okay?"

"You're on," said Terry. "I'll be there. But I'll be glad when this is done and dusted. Have you thought how to get her and Mike to split up? Seems like that will also be tricky."

"No, not yet," said Richard. "Just leave that to me though. It'll be a work in progress. I'm sure I'll think of something. Got to rush, mate. 9.30am on 29th. See you then." And with that, the conversation came to an abrupt close.

CHAPTER XII

After receiving Richard's last email confirming the meeting set up for 29th May, Emma felt that she'd made excellent progress, especially considering where she felt just a few weeks earlier, off the back of the incredibly sparse information she'd gleaned from her mom. At the same time, she felt the current situation was down to her inner resilience. Mike was supportive, but she felt only up to a point. It was as if no one else understood what it really meant to her. It was alright for her mom and Mike. No doubt they took it completely for granted that they knew who their true biological parents were as they grew up. It's not until you don't have that knowledge that you realise what you're missing.

Although she felt very relieved that a meeting was now set up, she still reflected on what she'd learned from her efforts. A medical student who studied at Edinburgh University. She felt an inner sense of pride that she shared genes from someone intelligent enough to have studied medicine. Given all her recent sleuthing efforts she was really 'in the groove'. She went back to her computer and decided to resume her activities armed with her newfound knowledge. Starting with a quick blanket search of 'Edinburgh University' she marvelled at the scope of the internet, a facility that she took for granted, given, in part, she'd never known a world without the internet. Still, that search found millions of matching records. She quickly refined her search a few times and, before long she hit upon a site that provided details and records for Edinburgh University alumni. She wasn't that familiar with the term 'alumni', but she guessed it referred to past graduates. Having clicked a few links, she was viewing images of past graduates, proudly holding their degree certificates. Of course, she still faced some limitations. Ideally, she was looking for a 'Nick' … or 'Nicholas'. But she still didn't know his last name. And she had no idea of the year of his graduation, although she used some nous to narrow down her search. A basic educated guess suggested to her that he'd probably be aged at least 50 now … and more probably closer to 60 or so … Through a simple process of extrapolation, she decided that somewhere around 1980 was a reasonable starting year, so she started looking at records two to three years either side of 1980. She was still somewhat surprised at the number of such alumni and before too long it began to feel like a somewhat onerous task. She did find several individual and group photos that she pored over intensely, believing that she may well be seeing the first image of her biological father, admittedly from when he was considerably younger than his current age. Some of the group photos didn't list the individuals by name, which made things tricky. However, there were quite a few photos of named individuals. Her heart skipped a beat whenever she found a 'Nicholas' – and she'd found several. What a shame she didn't yet have his last name. She'd just have to be patient, she figured, and wait to meet him on 29th May.

Emma also recalled that both Mike's father, Richard and his Uncle Dennis had both studied medicine. She had no idea where, although she had some very vague recollection that Mike may have mentioned something about Scotland in the past. She made a mental note to quiz him on this. Who knows, his father might have also studied at Edinburgh and maybe around a similar time. At the same time, she realised her mind was starting to work overtime.

In the following two weeks she did her best to concentrate on her studies and, in between, there was always the swimming for some alternative activity. She saw Mike at the swimming sessions a few times too and at the weekend they also met up to go for a drive into the countryside. It was during this trip that she quizzed Mike about his dad. "So ... didn't you mention something about your dad studying medicine up in Scotland?" she enquired.

"Yes, I don't recall how much I shared, but yes, he did ... he was at Edinburgh University."

"Really?" quizzed Emma, suddenly excited to have found this being confirmed.

"When was he there?" she continued.

"Why are you so interested in my dad's education all of a sudden?"

"Oh, just call it female curiosity" she responded in a slightly mischievous voice. She gave Mike a slightly coy smile, so he knew she was half teasing him. "No, just, given my own interest in nursing I've been looking at various University brochures and, well, I often find myself seeing Medicine also listed in some of these prospectuses. It must be great to be so brainy and have the luxury of being able to study anything. Medicine's so competitive anyway. There's no way I'd be up to anything like that!"

"Hey, don't beat yourself up," said Mike. "Nursing's an honourable profession to go into. Not everyone's cut out to be a doctor. Plus, it isn't all glamour like they portray on a whole load of medical dramas."

"Oh, I know that," said Emma. "It just must have been great for your dad to pursue that ambition and accomplish everything he has done in that competitive field". She was conscious of still wanting to prise out some idea of when Richard had done his medical studies, so she continued ..."so when was it he was at Edinburgh?"

"Oh, not sure, to be honest" said Mike, but he's nearly 60 now, so, just working back, A levels at 18 ... so, well, must have been around 40 years ago". She wasn't going to press Mike any more on the matter. That was good enough for her needs, she thought. She also didn't want to share any more, at least not for the present, about her connection with Nick Rawlings either with Mike, or her mom. No, she'd decided that that could wait until after she'd met up with the guy on 29th May.

Armed with the additional information she'd gleaned from Mike she did revert to her search on the Edinburgh University alumni site, and now she had the approximate year she narrowed down her search accordingly. She quickly found herself revisiting similar parts of the site that she'd visited before, but her earlier scattergun approach was now somewhat more focused. Again, she hit on some group photos and some individual photos. At some point during this search, she clicked on one group photo of medical graduates and there he was. Mike's Dad! Of course, he looked a fair bit younger, but then it was from some 40 years ago. But the face and his smile gave him away. He was in a group of maybe 10-12 graduates, and she glimpsed briefly across the group. How proud they all looked.

CHAPTER XIII

The morning of Sat 29th May

Terry Parker woke early. He'd had a very restless night's sleep, struggling to get the idea of the meeting with Emma out of his head. He was secretly worried. What if she asked him some tricky questions, he didn't feel equipped to answer? His only solace lay in reminding himself of Richard's reassurance. Richard was, indeed, a good friend, and had been for many years. Yes, he'd just have to go with the flow. He'd given more thought than usual to his attire for the day, doubtless due to his upcoming meeting with Emma. While he didn't want to dress too formally, at the same time, he wanted to at least appear as if he'd made an effort. He felt sure that not only Emma, but also Richard, would approve. He had on a freshly laundered white collared shirt and a casual, but smart jacket, tidy looking jeans, and some brown leather brogue shoes. After finishing his breakfast, he decided to make tracks. Richard had suggested meeting up at his house around 9.30am, but Terry was leaving nothing to chance, and he set off sufficiently early to reach Richard half an hour earlier. The drive was a pleasant one, across some of the bucolic rolling Yorkshire countryside and he caught occasional glimpses of high fells in the distance, signalling his growing proximity to Cumbria's Lake District. Sure enough, he made excellent time and, when he was just a few miles away from Richard's house he pulled into a lay-by and phoned Richard.

Richard picked up: "Richard White speaking".

"Richard, hi, it's Terry here. Listen, I'm about 15 minutes away. I just wanted to check the coast's clear. The rest of your family are out, right?"

"Hi Terry" he said. His tone had immediately transformed into one that was warmer and more effusive once he realised it was Terry. "Great to hear you and yes, I'm here on my own right now, so I look forward to seeing you very soon. It'll be great to catch up!"

"Okay, thanks Richard, see you in a bit," and he ended the call.

He knew that Richard was happy he'd agreed to play ball.

A short while later he pulled up at Richard's house and made his way to the front door. He rang the bell and Richard was there within seconds.

"Terry!!! Who's a smart looking gent on a Saturday morning?! Great to see you, come on in!" He gave Terry a hug.

They both walked down the hallway with Richard leading him into the lounge. "So, what'll it be, tea, coffee – or something a little stronger?"

Terry was certainly keen to opt for the latter, after all, he'd probably be having a coffee with Emma when they met up.

"Sure" said Terry, "a Scotch will be fine. But I am driving so just make it a small one".

Richard fixed two drinks, both small Scotches and handed one to Terry.

They both sat down. Terry pondered over the Scotch for a few seconds, almost massaging the glass in his hand, before quickly downing it on one.

"Feel better, for that?" quizzed Richard.

"A little" said Terry, as he suddenly felt the warmth of the alcohol hitting the back of his throat.

"Listen" said Richard. "I told you, this is going to be easy. Keep it all simple and high level. You remember the plan, don't you? It's not difficult. There's not much to remember. Basically, the meeting's a one off, you're soon retiring to the South Coast and, well, just play it cool. You'll be fine. Trust me. They continued with more small talk and then Richard once more went over the main points as a final reminder to Terry. "Right" he said a few moments later, "all ready, then?"

"As ready as I'll ever be!" With that, Terry got up and handed Richard his empty glass. "I'd better make tracks. Wish me luck."

"Trust me on this, you'll be fine. I'm going out myself shortly but give me a call once you're through just to let me know how it went, okay?".

"Sure thing Richard. Will do." And with that he walked into the hallway and to the front door. He made one last turn back to Richard and just winked. And then he walked to his car, got in and drove off. The traffic was quite light, and he made good time. In less than 10 minutes he found himself on the outskirts of the town. He parked in one of the smaller pay and display car parks, paid the requisite fee for an hour and started walking into the town centre. He knew where the Costa store was located, which was just a couple of minutes' away. He quickly glanced at his watch. It was 10.18am so he'd be several minutes early. He decided to browse in one or two shop windows en route to eat up one or two extra minutes. On one such occasion he suddenly caught glimpse of his own reflection in the window. His face was clearly visible. He saw the face of a worried looking middle aged man returning his gaze. He forced himself to smile slightly and mentally reminded himself to relax. He sensed some tension in his shoulders and made a conscious effort to tense and then relax his shoulder and neck muscles several times whilst taking a few slow deep breaths. He continued walking and could see the Costa store about 100 yards away. He wondered whether Emma was already there. Or maybe she was in the street (?) She could be just a few yards away for all he knew! He quickly looked around to check. The town centre was now becoming quite busy although he quickly reassured himself that she was not in sight. He quickly reached into his pocket where he kept the snapshot image Richard had provided. He studied her image for a few seconds, before placing it back in his pocket and then walked purposefully across to the Costa store. The glass windows enabled a view into the store, but it was quite a long narrow store. Emma could be in there already but out of sight towards the back of the store, he thought. He walked in through the main door and quickly perused the occupants. If she was in the store, she'd have to be in the back section. He could roughly see towards the back section and didn't see anyone remotely matching Emma. He therefore reckoned she hadn't yet arrived. He was third in line in the queue and, every few seconds while he was waiting, he found himself turning round to check that she hadn't walked in right behind him. It only took a couple of minutes for him to get served. "What can we do for you this morning Sir?" asked the young waitress behind the counter. He guessed that she was perhaps about the same age as Emma. A student making a bit of extra cash to get by, he thought.

"Oh, just a regular latte, please?" he said. The waitress didn't reply but merely turned to start preparing his drink.

"Nick?" uttered a female voice from behind him. He quickly turned around and there stood Emma. He checked himself, aware that he'd responded in the way someone might have done so if *any* name had been called out, rather than if his name really was 'Nick'. He forced a smile and hoped it looked sincere. "Ah, you must be ... Emma?" She nodded. "Yes, it's me."

Although she couldn't be described as a stereotypical stunner, she was nevertheless a very pleasant looking young lady who met his gaze. She was perhaps a few inches shorter than him, so in fact quite tall – maybe around 5ft 9inches. He guessed that she, too, had taken some care with her dress sense for the meeting. She wore smart well-fitting denim jeans that showed off her youthful figure and this was nicely complemented by a powder blue blouse underneath a medium blue padded jacket that was half unzipped. He thought he detected a slight whiff of perfume. He couldn't be sure but, if he was to guess, it certainly smelt like a more expensive brand, possibly Chanel. He wondered if she'd maybe snatched a quick spray from her mother but quickly realised his mind was working overtime. Relax, said an inner voice to himself. She extended a hand, somewhat awkwardly, almost as if she wasn't sure whether to have offered to shake his hand or hug him. Dutifully, his hand met hers and they shook hands. "Pleased to finally meet you, Emma. I've just placed my order. Please ... what can I get you? My treat."

"Oh, thanks. Can I just have a skinny latte, please?"

"Sure. Why don't you see if you can find a table? It's not overly busy but the tables are starting to get filled. The back of the store might be our best bet. They seem to be taken right here near the counter."

With that, Emma nodded in agreement and started walking towards the back of the store. Terry watched her walk away. This is it, he thought. His mind was racing a little, mainly around reflecting on her appearance and thinking what similarities he could see that might provide a clue that she was in fact the progeny from Richard's sperm donation from all those years before. Certainly, she seemed tall. Richard was maybe a couple of inches taller than him, which he suspected could explain where she got her height from. It wasn't a dead giveaway looking at her face, although the general cast of features, complexion and hair colouring did relate. Richard had dark brown hair and blue eyes; Emma was more a dark blonde although she too had blue eyes. His own hair was dark, almost black in fact, although unlike Richard his own hairline had already started to recede. And his own eyes were brown.

While he waited for both drinks to be prepared, he glanced again at his watch. 10.25am. They were both early. Emma no doubt keen: he was simply nervous. The drinks were placed on the counter. He picked them up and turned to walk towards the back of the store. Emma had found a small table in the far corner that was backed up to a wall. To one side of the table was the back window of the store with a view out to a narrow walkway courtyard. Terry placed Emma's drink on the table in front of her before seating himself opposite her.

Emma immediately began speaking. "So, Nick ... is it okay to call you Nick?"

"Oh, yes, sure," said Nick.

"I just wanted to start by saying thanks again so much for agreeing to meet up. You don't know how weird this feels to me. To finally meet the person who ... well, helped bring me into this world, and whose genes I share!"

"Yes, I suppose when you put it like that, it's, well, quite profound I suppose", said Terry. He'd thought over this moment many times over since Richard had broached the topic and he'd agreed to help. As something of a strategy in his mind he thought it probably made good sense to try to control the conversation as much as possible, though he acknowledged that that could also prove somewhat challenging. "And, just to put you fully in the picture, when I, ahem, took part in this … process, well, it was quite a common thing that we all did at the time."

"Yes, I was wondering a bit about that." She paused momentarily before continuing. "So, you were a medical student … up in Edinburgh?

"Yes, that's right. You're quite an accomplished sleuth I see."

"Well, yes, that was what they more or less implied at the Clinic where I first enquired". Terry sensed that she'd inadvertently lowered her voice and leaned in slightly towards him when she mentioned the Clinic. He liked that touch. "But the information was pretty sparse to be honest. And then there was the email, which I thought was … well, pretty unusual."

Terry was prepared for this and had rehearsed his spiel several times over beforehand. "Ah, yes, of course, I've had that email for many years now. There was little in the way of guidance for how to construct an email back then, so it just seemed natural to use the first part of my surname 'Rawlings' that also spells out the simple word 'raw'. I also suspected it might make it quite memorable, too". He smiled at this point and Emma returned the smile. It was only now that he could suddenly see she had cute dimples in her cheeks which added to her general appeal. Yet another feature she'd probably acquired from Richard.

"I'm so glad that you responded".

"Oh, no problem, although, as I said in the email, when I took part in this … er … process, I had no intention or anticipation that I'd end up being in touch with, well, someone like yourself. I think it's important for you to realise that we … me and my peers, routinely took part as much in a quest to effectively help support those individuals looking to start a family. It might surprise you to know just how difficult it is for many adults and the process itself is fraught with challenges. It's certainly no guarantee of producing a baby. The sheer numbers out there trying would no doubt surprise a lot of people. You, or certainly your mother can certainly consider yourself to be one of the lucky ones."

Terry started to feel a little more comfortable now he'd been able to expand on a topic about which he felt reasonably conversant. He paused to sip his coffee. This provided a suitable opportunity for her to speak.

"So, I don't want to pry too much, but I'm keen to know some more about you if that's okay." Terry was half expecting a little bit of amateur interrogation from Emma, but the next question she threw at him was not one he had anticipated. "But before I ask you a bit more about a few biological questions I'd thought up, I did just want to ask you if you've ever heard of a man called Richard White?"

"Richard White?" Terry repeated back to her, half hoping to buy a couple of seconds breathing space before responding. He sensed that his initial shock at being asked had already translated into some subtle body language giveaways. Maybe an initial look of surprise. His mind raced. He could simply deny, but she'd obviously already tracked Richard down as a fellow medical student from Edinburgh University from around the same time. He decided to keep things as simple as possible.

"Richard White" he said again, only more slowly and deliberate this time, as if trying to claw back at some distant memory. "Well now, there's a blast from the past!", he said finally. Yes, I remember Richard. We studied together at Edinburgh. We were both medical students. Why do you ask?" He sincerely hoped his own question had appeared genuine.

Emma's eyes lit up. "Ha, what a coincidence" she proclaimed. "I'm only going out with his son!"

"Really?" said Terry, again hoping his vocal sincerity level hadn't dropped. "Well, well, now, yes, that is quite a coincidence."

"Do ... did you know him well?" quizzed Emma.

"Oh, quite well, I suppose. I mean we spent several years up there in Edinburgh. He was one of several friends of mine at the time. We kept in touch for a while, but I haven't seen him in a while (he lied). It was a long time ago, of course. To follow up and as if to continue showing some genuine interest he said "and ... Richard ... is he well?"

"Oh, yes, I suppose so," said Emma. "I see him fairly regularly when I'm round at his place."

Terry looked at Emma and pondered over the fact that, less than an hour earlier he'd been standing in Richard's house. Whatever would she think if she knew that?! Having addressed this topic, he decided it'd be good to move on. He was hoping for no more similarly challenging curveball questions and tried to move the conversation on.

"Well, please do pass on my best wishes when you next see him. I don't have long to speak with you this morning as I mentioned. Sorry to press a little but you, er ... mentioned some other scientific or biological questions you had on your mind?"

"Oh, yes. Let's see, I mean, I've been thinking about, I don't know, maybe any genetic things that might be of use or just be of general interest. I am studying biology at school. I'm doing my A levels. We've been covering some basic genetics. Apart from some of the more obvious things like hair colour and eye colour – which, it looks like I may well have inherited more from my mom". She paused briefly and smiled as she looked at him intently. He briefly returned the smile in acknowledgement. "But I was wondering about maybe things like allergies and stuff." She intoned the sentence, so it sounded like a non-rhetorical question. "Is there anything you're aware of that might be good for me to know?"

Terry's mind was now highly attuned. His response was already being formulated although he was constantly on guard given the need for him to remember that Emma's question wasn't anything about *his* genetic identity, but rather Richard's! He mentally steeled himself to be cautious.

His own genetic 'footprint' would ordinarily have lent itself quite handily for a ready reply but relating to Richard's biological profile was something far more challenging. Racking his brain, he thought back to the years he and Richard had spent together in early adulthood. He couldn't recall anything of note such as particular susceptibility to certain medical conditions such as seasonal rhinitis or hay fever. He was already conscious of Emma's dimples, which, in all probability she had probably inherited from Richard. Also, given the various hair and eye colour anomalies he was keen to help redress the balance a little. Briefly, his own mind went back to some of those early lessons on genetics at medical school.

"Well now. Let me think about that for a minute" he said, stalling a little for time. There was some distant memory that he was grasping back from his own memory bank and, just then, it suddenly came to him. Tongue rolling! He still remembered the lecturer running through a variety of commonly inherited traits and tongue rolling was one of them. Importantly, to demonstrate this to the class all those years ago, he'd stuck out his own tongue and rolled it for them all to see. He'd then proclaimed that this was one such example of the manifestation of a dominant gene before asking the entire class to try to do the same. Everyone had done so and of course, everyone then looked around at their peers to observe who could ... and who couldn't roll their tongues.

At the time, Terry had been sat a short distance away from Richard and he distinctly recalled them both catching each other's eyes, both with their tongues clearly protruding from their mouths – and 'rolled'!!

Terry's face developed as warm a smile as he could muster as he carefully began his response, almost as if he had been speaking to one of his patients. He thought he'd provide a fuller general response so he could lead up to the tongue rolling trait. "Oh, Emma, there's not much to say on that point, which maybe you'll find somewhat reassuring. Of course, as you'll no doubt be aware, genetics is an extraordinarily complex branch of biology. While some traits and characteristics might sound obvious such as blood groups, hair, and eye colour etc, there are many, many traits that are almost impossible to predict with any degree of accuracy. That said, I, er, couldn't help but notice those dimples of yours. Maybe you inherited those from your mother as I certainly wasn't blessed with that trait myself.

"Oh" Emma laughed. "No, that's funny. I certainly don't get them from my mom". Terry mused to himself that it was very probable she had indeed acquired them from Richard.

"Well, there you go, you see. Genetic complexities at work. But here's one that might amuse you. Can you, by chance, do this?" With that, he gently pulled out his tongue and rolled it. Of course, he had no idea whether Emma would be able to do so, but he felt there was a reasonable chance that she could, especially given he knew that Richard possessed the ability to do so. Emma looked at him with a puzzled expression on her face and slowly stuck out her tongue. And she rolled it! They both withdrew their tongues and laughed.

"Well, you see there. That's a fairly common example of a dominant gene at play." Now he felt he'd got her onside he was quick to continue. "No" he said, "other than that, genetically I'm pretty unremarkable. No obvious predispositions to allergies and the like". To lighten the mood still further, he ended with "and no history of any mental health problems, though maybe some of my patients might beg to differ". He waited a moment before smiling. Emma laughed.

They both drank some more of their coffees.

Terry paused to look through the window outside the shop. A goodly number of people were now milling around. The sun was shining and there were blue cloudless skies above. He was still conscious of making mention of his impending retirement plans and relocation as he'd discussed at length with Richard.

"It looks like it's turning into a nice day, although it was a bit fresh when I got up this morning" he said, to keep a little of the small talk going. Secretly, in the short time he'd been speaking with Emma he was impressed by what he saw. A young intelligent woman with a very pleasing manner and a good sense of humour. He had certainly warmed to her. If she had been his genetic offspring, he would have been keen to continue getting to know her better.

At the same time, he wanted to honour Richard's instruction and leave her in no doubt as to there being no prospect of any further direct contact between them.

"Yes" said Emma. Almost as if she was reading his own mind, it was Emma who next raised the topic. "So, Nick, you said about this just being a one-off meeting … was there any particular reason for not wanting to ever meet up again?"

For a moment, just a moment, he considered the option of continuing to meet Emma and he was briefly tempted to agree, but he quickly checked himself. This wasn't a decision he had any freedom to call. He was doing an old pal a favour. That was the agreement.

"Well," he started. "First, be reassured, this is absolutely nothing against you, Emma. Only, I had no inclination of even *this* meeting taking place. I mean think about it. For all I know there could be several people around who could be the result of, this ... process, from all those years ago. As I mentioned briefly in our emails, I was under the belief that my records at the Clinic were confidential. I confess, I'm aware that it's now considered totally legitimate for people such as yourself to track down their biological donors as you indeed have done. In addition, there's an additional purely pragmatic element as well which I hadn't yet mentioned. I'm nearing retirement myself and I'm going to be relocating down to the South Coast. So, even if I'd wanted to maintain any further physical contact, any actual meetings would also prove to be particularly challenging. It's just going to be a lot simpler to not have any future pressures around meeting up in person."

"Oh!" said Emma, clearly surprised at hearing this update. He could see she looked a little hurt. The earlier smiles were replaced with a distinct frown.

"Well, what about email contact. Would that still be okay?" And before he had chance to respond she added, "I wouldn't be any bother, really. I don't have any desire to pester you or anything. Just occasional catch ups maybe?"

Terry considered this to be a curveball question and not one that he'd had any hope of rehearsing with Richard. Thinking quickly, he responded with "Hmm. I'm not sure. Look I don't want to say an absolute no. Let's say it's a definite maybe as of right now. Let me at least mull this over for a day or two, okay?" He flashed his best smile to show that he was sincere. Emma smiled back.

Another, and potentially much larger curveball was just about to hit the pair of them: one that neither one of them could have anticipated. Out of the corner of his peripheral vision he caught a glimpse of a figure approaching the shop from outside on the other side of the adjacent glass window. He looked up and surveyed the approaching figure. A young man, probably in his early 20s with athletic build and a neat, cropped haircut. The man's gaze was directed more towards Emma than him. Emma had also spotted the approaching stranger at about the same time as Terry. She immediately stood up at the table, waved her hand briefly, smiled a broad smile, started miming something that was clearly unintelligible and used her arm to motion the gentleman to come inside the shop. Terry guessed straightaway who this man was and thanked his good fortune that the entrance to the shop was around the front, thus providing them both with a few vital seconds to discuss the situation.

Emma spoke quickly and excitedly, "that's Mike, my boyfriend."

Terry, too, responded quickly. "I don't want him knowing who I am, I mean, why we're here, ok?!" Emma could tell by the tone of his voice that he was serious.

"Leave it to me, Nick. It's okay to just call you by your first name though … I can make out you're a careers adviser or something. It'll be fine. You know I'm looking at doing nursing. I had no idea Mike would be in town this morning. We're meeting up later this afternoon."

With that, Terry looked towards the front of the shop and could see Mike approaching them both. He was about 10 yards away. He could tell straightaway that he was Richard's son. It was almost like looking at the Richard he'd known at medical school. He smiled a winning smile in Emma's direction. Oh God, he thought. He also had Richard's dimples! Suddenly he could see some definite similarities between Mike and Emma. He felt a definite sinking feeling inside but felt now was the time he must keep calm.

"Emma! Surprised to see you here," said Mike. They embraced warmly and kissed each other on the cheek. "So, are you going to introduce me to your friend?" With that, his gaze turned towards Terry. Terry stood up and they shook hands. "Hi" said Terry, taking the initial lead. "I'm Nick. Just giving Emma here some er ... careers advice." "Oh, okay," said Mike. Thankfully, Emma then picked up the prompt from there. "Yes" said Emma, turning her attention firmly towards Mike. "Remember I told you I was looking over those prospectuses. Well, I got talking to the Careers adviser guy at school, you know, Mr Sullivan. Quite by chance he said he knew a close colleague who's a Nursing Tutor – well, Nick's into Medicine big time, but he's got Nursing Tutor background too. He offered to put me in touch with him and Nick suggested we meet up for coffee. It was all last-minute stuff that happened yesterday. He had some time this morning so ... here we are! Otherwise, I'd have mentioned to you." Terry was again impressed by how Emma was handling the situation. Before he could interject again, Emma continued "We're nearly done here anyway, Nick needs to leave soon. Hey, we're still on for this afternoon, yes?"

Mike responded "Yes, sure. I was lucky to spot you, I just needed to get to the bank quickly to sort out a transaction with them. Having some hassle with my card." His eyes looked heavenwards. "Got to run." He then turned briefly back to Terry. "Nice meeting you." With that, he turned back to Emma, they hugged and kissed before he turned and left the shop. "See you later!" he said as he turned and walked away.

"Wow!" said Terry, "I wasn't expecting to bump into your boyfriend! Thanks for handling the conversation. So, I'm a Nursing Tutor Careers Adviser, then?" He smiled broadly. Emma laughed. "Yes, did you like that bit, Nick?" Nevertheless, he could still feel his pulse racing a little. By any stretch of the imagination, it had been a close call. He decided to press a little further. "So, how long have you two been together?"

"Oh, it's over a year now, but we knew one another for a few years before then from the swimming club where we both train."

"Keen swimmers, eh? And ... I don't mean to pry but ..." he paused for a second before continuing "Is it serious?"

Emma smiled, "Yes, we think so. Mike's at Loughborough University studying Economics, so he's a bit ahead of me, so we tend to get together at weekends right now."

"Well, I wish you luck" was all Terry felt he could say. Inside he felt a sadness, not only for Emma, who, presently, was simply ignorant of the wider picture, but also for Richard, who faced this ongoing dilemma. He didn't envy his good friend's plight.

"Listen" he said, glancing at his watch, "I do really need to get moving myself". He finished off the remnants of his coffee.

"Yes, me too" said Emma, although he surmised that she would have liked to have carried on with the conversation if that option had remained.

Terry stood up, as too did Emma. "It's been very pleasant meeting you" he said, "but, like I said ..." he tailed off without finishing the sentence. "I promise I'll think things over and get back to you by email soon, okay?"

"Yes, sure, thanks again, Nick."

With that, he reached out and gave her a friendly hug, feeling a little genuine affection towards her after their brief meeting.

"I'll be in touch, okay?" Another brief pause and then he said "Bye." And with that, he turned and walked out of the shop.

He started walking along the main street but having taken only a dozen or so paces, curiosity got the better of him and he turned to look around. There, stood stationary outside the shop was Emma, looking straight back at him. He felt strangely self-conscious almost as if she was still checking him out, but he checked himself and rationally believed that his mind was simply working overtime again. He raised an arm to provide a brief wave goodbye and Emma reciprocated. He turned away and continued walking briskly. He turned into the main market square. There were quite a few people around. He made another couple of turns down one alleyway and then another before pausing outside a shop window. That was a close call, he thought to himself. He took out a handkerchief from his pocket and gently mopped his brow. Yes, he had started to sweat! He replaced the handkerchief in his pocket and continued to make his way back to his car. Once inside his car he felt in a safer place. He located his phone and tapped in Richard's number …

CHAPTER XIV

Terry heard the number ring twice before it was picked up at the other end. "Richard White speaking."

"Richard, it's me, Terry. Listen, we've got a problem!"

"A problem? How do you mean?"

"I've just finished the meeting with Emma. We should talk again. Are you free again, I'll be driving past your house again in 15 mins, would that work?"

"Yes, sure," said Richard. "Now you've got me concerned, can't you tell me briefly the issue?"

"No, it'll be easier to discuss once I reach your place. See you in a bit." With that, he ended the call, threw his phone onto the passenger seat, started the engine, and pulled away. Fifteen minutes later he was again pulling up on Richard's drive. He got out and walked up to the front door. Richard must have heard him arrive and was already opening the door as he reached it.

"Come on in," said Richard. Together they walked through the hallway and back into the same room they'd occupied earlier that same morning.

"You haven't got another Scotch, have you?" said Terry. Richard could tell that he wasn't in a joking mood.

"Sure" said Richard. He quickly fixed Terry the drink and handed it to him as he continued. "So, tell me. How did it go? What happened?"

"Well," Terry started. "It was all proceeding quite well to begin with. But I was hit with a couple of bombshells. First, she asked me if I knew you?!" He swallowed the Scotch in one gulp.

"Me?!" said Richard.

"Yes. Clearly, she's been digging around on that old Edinburgh University website. She's put two and two together and, well, she's come up with 4!"

"What did you say?"

"What could I say? I could hardly say I'd never heard of you, could I? There are probably old images that show us together in the same year. It'd sound incredulous to have said that I didn't know you from Adam, now, wouldn't it? I just skimmed over it and gave her some vague old bull about us being old colleagues but that we'd largely lost contact with each other over the years. But that's not the worst."

"What, there's more?" said Richard.

"Yes. We were getting near the end and then who should walk along outside the shop but your son – Mike! Of course, once he'd spotted her inside, he came right up to the window, and she motioned him to come inside."

"Oh no!" said Richard. "Did … he … recognise you?"

"Well, who knows? Honestly, I don't think so. I was racking my brain to try and figure out how long ago it was he saw me. Thankfully when we've been meeting up these past few years it's been just the two of us. But wasn't there that GP Conference we attended where we had that additional social gathering? Mind you, that's got to be more than 10 years ago now."

"Yes, I think you're right, Terry. Of course, Mike was just a young lad at the time. He probably saw a good number of my GP colleagues at the time so it's possible he simply wouldn't remember you. Plus, of course, he wouldn't have known you this morning as Terry, would he … I'm guessing you or Emma would have mentioned you as Nick – yes?"

"Yes, that's right. In fact, Emma was incredibly good you know … right on the spur of the moment she concocted some crazy story about me being some nursing tutor careers adviser. I'm sure Mike bought into it. She's a smart cookie. But this still leaves me feeling very uneasy. What if Mike now starts digging … I mean, with Emma. Especially if he's got any inkling that I look vaguely familiar to him. Think about it, lads change a lot in appearance between the ages of 10 and 20. At our age we don't tend to change that much from our 50s to 60s." They both fell silent for a short while as if meditating on this newfound development and wondering what best to do next.

"Well," said Terry finally, "how do you want to handle this?"

"For right now, I suggest we just let things lie and play it by ear. I can see how Mike is later. Just see if he happens to mention anything that might indicate he's clocked you. If we're fortunate we may be okay: if for any reason he has any suspicions, we can cross that bridge …"

"I guess so," said Terry. "I still feel very uneasy though. Emma's been digging and Mike may have suspicions now. If they get talking to one another. It might not be pretty."

"You're just painting a gloomy picture. Let's ride this one out and see how things go, okay?"

"Well, there's not much more we can do is there? Look, I need to get going anyway. Keep me posted, yes. Anything at all." Terry moved to the hallway and started making his way to the front door.

"Of course," said Richard. "And hey, thanks again for today. I do appreciate it. And look, we'll probably be fine.

We may just be over thinking this." Terry left and Richard closed the door after him. Inwardly, he was as concerned, if not more so, than Terry.

CHAPTER XV

Later that same day.

Mike and Emma had met up, as agreed, and driven out to The Helme, a local high spot close to Kendal where they could enjoy the fresh air together. They had just started walking and immediately continued chatting. Often this was an opportunity to talk about myriad things that concerned them, Emma's studies, Richard's studies, swimming, plans for the Summer etc. Before too long though the subject of Emma's morning meeting naturally came up in the conversation.

"So, how did that meeting go with Nick, was it, this morning?"

"Yes, it went really well thanks," said Emma. Given the circumstances, she felt that she didn't want to dwell on the topic too long, especially because the more granular details she'd discovered from digging into the details of who her biological father was, thus far, kept discreet.

"Only, there was something about him. Can't quite put my finger on it, but I thought he looked kind of familiar. Does he live locally?" quizzed Mike.

Again, Emma wanted to tread carefully. Not to give too much away, at least for the present. "Not from Kendal, no. I think he lives over in Yorkshire so not that far away. He's a GP right now, but I guess he's just got a lot of medical knowledge and I gather he's been involved with nursing communities in the past." (She felt the need to embellish her response a little, so the last element was an addition which she made up to suit her earlier narrative). She carried on "familiar? In what way? You think you've seen him before?"

"Yes, possibly, said Mike. But I can't for the life of me think where. And I don't think it's anyone I've seen recently, assuming it is someone I've seen before. Maybe from a while back. But then, maybe he just looks a bit like someone I've met before."

"Well,", said Emma. "He is a GP now. Maybe he's been at some Doctor gatherings that your dad attended in the past. Something like that, maybe?"

"Yes, that's a thought. I might just ask my dad if he's ever heard of the guy. What was his name again ... Nick what?"

"Nick Rawlings". Again, Emma didn't want to disclose much more currently. She still had her own thoughts about wanting to do some further investigative work on the Edinburgh University alumni site she'd found some days earlier. In particular, she wanted to go back to some of those photos she'd seen. At the same time, it'd be interesting to hear back from Mike once he'd quizzed his dad, Richard. She also wanted to go back to social media in another attempt to locate Nick. Perhaps he was one of those people who simply didn't get involved with social media. That could explain her not finding him before when she'd taken a cursory look. The remainder of their walk progressed uneventfully. They soon got to chatting on other topics. Emma always loved walking up on the Helme. The panoramic view spread out to one side where Kendal town could clearly be seen, with the backdrop of the fells also clearly on view. Turning her gaze 90 degrees, she could also see the South Lakes estuary some 5 miles off into the distance. Walking here was always like the proverbial 'breath of fresh air' which she always felt to be beneficial.

Some hours later and, true to her word, she was there, searching through social media outlets looking for Nick Rawlings but the usual outlets proved to be very disappointing. Well, to qualify that a little, she soon discovered that the name Nick Rawlings must be one of the commonest names on the planet! She found numerous people with that name on social media, none of whom looked or sounded remotely like the Nick she'd met. She also tried a simple search on Google and found, pretty much, a similar finding. In fact, more than a million matching records. When she fine-tuned her search just down to images, again, there were seemingly plenty of matching records. She even found a professor, although without the 'g' in the spelling of the last name. She returned to the Edinburgh University alumni site and began sifting once more through the records. If only she could at least find an image of Nick, now she'd finally met him. She reverted to the photo she'd seen earlier that included Richard, Mike's Dad, in a group photo. This time she took more time to peruse the other members of the group. The images weren't crystal clear and more than a little grainy, but then, suddenly, she spotted him. There he was – Nick! At least she thought so. There were two rows of people in the photo. Richard was in the front row, two from the right and although she couldn't be sure, the person pictured in the back row four from the right bore a definite resemblance to Nick! A list of names appeared underneath the photo but, strangely, there was no Nick Rawlings! The names were listed in order from left to right, back row names first and then the front row. Richard was 10th along on that basis and, sure enough, counting along the list, the 10th name was Richard White. She went back to the back row names and, by the same logic, Nick was going to be the 8th name along in the list, but all she saw there for the 8th name listed was the name Terry Parker. How very odd, she thought. Maybe it was a mistake. She studied the image again. Maybe it was just someone who had an uncanny similarity to Nick. She went to a drawer in her chest of drawers and pulled open the second drawer down. In one corner was a small box filled with a variety of oddments. A small pair of scissors, a vanity mirror, and a map compass with a rectangular plastic base. She picked it up. Towards one end was a small circular magnifying glass. She went back to the alumni photo and studied Nick's image using the magnifying glass. It was certainly a heck of a coincidence if it proved not to be him. Admittedly, the image was taken decades ago, but she felt the likeness was uncanny. Surely it was him! She wondered if there was a mistake with the naming of the individuals, though she suspected that that did seem a long shot. Could it be that Nick Rawlings was in fact Terry Parker?! But why? Her sleuthing now took a sideways turn and she started trawling the internet and social media sites again, only this time searching for anyone named Terry Parker. She felt it was her bad luck again that the name 'Terry Parker', a little like 'Nick Rawlings' seemed to be an incredibly popular name so the searching, although superficially at least seemed to be very productive, the process still required significant painstaking efforts on her part to trawl through all the potentially matching records. After some time, although she found nothing likely on Facebook, Twitter, and Instagram, she did venture over to look on LinkedIn and there, she did find several matches, one of which did seem to be a close match. Certainly, the record she found was a GP currently, based out of Yorkshire. There were some gaps in the jigsaw for this person but crucially, it did show up his educational background and Edinburgh University was mentioned. Sadly, she couldn't see any image for this person on

LinkedIn, so she felt that, although the record potentially added substantially to her findings, at the same time, she didn't feel it was conclusive. Consequently, she still felt a great sense of confusion. She decided to wait and hear what Mike had to say after speaking with his dad.

Emma also picked up on other parts of the conversation she'd had with Nick (or was he Terry, now?) "… just how difficult it is for many adults … it's certainly no guarantee of producing a baby. The sheer numbers out there trying would no doubt surprise a lot of people. You, or certainly your mother can certainly consider yourself to be one of the lucky ones."

Consequently, this also prompted her to revisit the IVF internet sites. She was curious to put some numbers together in her head to gauge the scope of the IVF challenge. She quite quickly learned that Nick was certainly right on that score. From just a few years earlier, in 2018, she saw one statistic stating that more than 50,000 people were undergoing IVF: this was just in one year! In addition, as Nick had also stated, the chances of success were certainly not guaranteed, with people often trying the IVF process several times. Even then, the success rates were sometimes as low as 20-30%, although this seemed to be dependent on a variety of factors. She reflected on these figures for a while. 50,000 in just one year! A rough estimate told her that that number could quite easily equate to 1,000,000 over a 20-year period. Wow! She thought for a moment how many other young adults might be facing a similar situation to herself.

CHAPTER XVI

M ike arrived back home late afternoon and both his mom and Dad were in. His Mom was in the kitchen. It sounded like she was boiling the kettle. "Hi mom", he shouted through from the hallway. If you're making a pot can you make enough for me, please?"

His Mom, Sue, shouted back, "Sure, Mike, it'll be ready in a few mins. If you're in the lounge I'll bring it through. Richard, do you want one, too?"

"Thanks, mom" Mike shouted back.

"You must have read my mind," Richard responded after Mike. "Thanks!"

His Dad was in his study, a place where he spent, in Mike's eyes, far too long, poring over research papers. He went into the lounge and flopped down on the settee, mulling over what Emma had told him about Nick Rawlings. His Dad would probably take a break once his tea was made, and he guessed he'd come into the lounge to briefly check in with Mike. Sure enough, just a few minutes later, his mom emerged slowly into the lounge carrying two hot mugs of tea on a tray, one for herself and the other which she carefully handed to Mike. "Thanks Mom", he said as he took the mug from her.

"So, how's it going?" she said to Mike, "doing anything exciting later?"

"No, nothing really," said Mike. "I was in town earlier though and I did bump into Emma."

"Oh?" remarked Sue.

"Yes, she was meeting up with this bloke … some sort of careers adviser guy, giving her some tips and stuff on Nursing. He looked vaguely familiar to me. I gather he's a doctor now – over the border in Yorkshire somewhere. I was wondering if there was a chance he could be an old colleague of Dad's."

"He'll probably come in in a minute now he's got his tea." And sure enough, shortly afterwards he came into the lounge.

"Ooh, nice to have a bit of a break from the computer. Hi son, how's it going?"

"Yes, fine thanks," said Mike.

Sue chimed in, "Mike was just saying he might have bumped into one of your colleagues in town, this morning."

"Oh?" said Richard. He was at least somewhat primed for this conversation to crop up. He turned to Mike. "Who was that, then?"

"Oh, I was just telling Mom. I bumped into Emma in Costa this morning. She was having this meeting with a guy called Nick … Nick Rawlings, who was giving her some careers advice apparently – about her nursing aspirations. But I gather he's a GP, based over in Yorkshire somewhere. Turns out he did his medical degree up in Edinburgh around the same time as you, so naturally I was curious to know if you knew him?" Mike was being a little crafty, knowing that Nick had already confirmed that he knew Richard from those days, he'd deliberately couched the question in an open-ended manner to see how Richard would respond. He also kept to himself the fact that he looked vaguely familiar.

"Nick!" Richard felt well primed to speak with confidence at this point. "Yes, I remember Nick. We were good friends at Edinburgh. That's where we met. Well, what a small world." He carried on "in fact, it's just possible you might remember him from a long time back, Mike. You too, Sue!"

"Oh, don't include me in this," said Sue. "You've had so many GP colleagues and acquaintances over the years I doubt I'd remember half of them."

"Well, that adds up," said Mike. "Funny, but I mentioned something similar to Emma."

"Oh?" quizzed Richard, doing his best to maintain the acting pretence of being genuinely surprised.

"Yes. I was introduced to him, and I thought that there was something vaguely familiar about him."

"Good memory, Mike. Yes, back in the day I often used to attend conferences and the like. You might just have seen him on one or two of those occasions, although you'd have been a lot younger then. No doubt still in short trousers." Mike and Richard chuckled while Sue also had a warm smile of recollection on her face.

Richard now felt as if he was, once more, controlling the conversation with aplomb. "So, I suppose you didn't get much chance to chat with him, then?" He paused briefly before continuing … "I haven't seen him for quite a while. You just tend to lose touch as the years roll by."

"No", said Mike. "It was really very brief as I had to get to the bank. Like you say though. Heck of a coincidence!"

"Yes. The next time I see Emma, I must quiz her some more. Anyway, good to catch up with you Mike. Everything else going well?"

"Yes, fine thanks", said Mike.

"Well, no rest for the wicked. These medical journal articles won't review themselves." He turned towards Sue. "I'm just going to give it another hour or so and then call it a day. See you in a bit." And with that he turned to leave the lounge and return to his home study.

CHAPTER XVII

Later that same evening.

As much a courtesy, Mike texted Emma to provide her with an update of sorts.

Mike: Hey Emma, Spoke with my dad. He confirmed he knew Nick Rawlings who he studied alongside at Edinburgh. Just wanted to let you know. Love, Mike x

Emma saw the message but felt at this stage she might have hit on an interesting development from her searches earlier in the day. Consequently, she still wanted to keep things to herself for the present. There would be plenty of time to loop in Mike once she'd managed to get to the bottom of the name anomaly. Alternatively, she reckoned, if she felt she'd hit a complete roadblock she could also loop in Mike at that point, and they could both try to figure out best next steps.

Emma: Thanks for checking, Mike. Good to know. Speak soon. Love, Emma x

Emma remained intensely puzzled by the apparent name anomaly. She racked her brain. What could possibly explain the anomaly? Maybe his real name is Terry Parker, and he changed his name from Nick Rawlings by deed poll. But why? And why would he want to continue telling her that Nick was still his real name? What possible reason could he have for wanting to conceal his real identity as Terry Parker? And, if his real name was Terry Parker, what role did Richard play, if any, in all of this? He seemed to know him as Nick Rawlings too. Ultimately, with various permutations going round and round in her head, she considered that maybe, just maybe, Nick was lying. But again, why? And would this also imply that Richard, too, was also lying? If Terry had changed his name, for whatever reason, some time ago, maybe Richard wasn't informed about this at the time, hence him still recalling his old acquaintance as 'Nick'. Something clearly wasn't adding up and she felt she had to work out what to do next.

Her mind went back briefly to the GP record she'd found for a Terry Parker in Yorkshire. That seemed the best place to start. She retrieved the details once again. The GP practice was based in Settle, a small town on the Western edge of Yorkshire. She could phone maybe. But what would she say? 'Can I speak to Dr Parker?' She envisaged the conversation. These days you typically got fobbed off by some receptionist and it could be tricky to get to speak with a GP. She surmised that it also didn't help with her not being registered with this practice either. No doubt some overzealous receptionist would first ask her name. And if she divulged that, would that then reach Terry Parker and, he'd then have the option of simply not speaking to her. This, of course, assumed that Terry Parker was the same Nick Rawlings she'd met in Kendal. That was effectively what she was trying to establish. But maybe she could give a false name? Maybe she could imply that she'd soon be moving to the area and was therefore looking to register with a new GP. But then in that case, surely there'd be no actual need to speak directly with the Doctor. Every which way her mind turned seemed to foster new waves of frustration. The receptionist would probably handle any initial, speculative enquiries. Maybe she could say she was looking to move to the area in the next week or two, but that she had an actual medical matter that she wanted to discuss with the Doctor. Yes, that was a possibility. She felt that, if she could at least hear Dr Parker's voice, she'd then have a particularly good idea if it was indeed the Nick Rawlings man she'd met. Her other thought was to simply visit Settle, find the GP practice and try to see if she could get a glimpse of him. But then Settle, while not being a huge distance away from Kendal, would still be an awkward, time-consuming journey to make using public transport. If only she had a car!! Her plan was slowly forming, and she decided that she'd try phoning first and, if she derived little success from that route, then she felt that the time was right to share more about this whole saga with Mike. Given Mike drove a car she'd then convince him to drive over to Settle with her. It'd be a nice little trip as well. She reckoned it would probably take less than an hour to drive there, compared with perhaps a couple of hours if she was to resort to using public transport. Yes, that's what she'd do!

She found the number for the surgery quite quickly, but she wanted to ensure she had her story 'straight' once she got connected. She also decided she'd need one or two back up plans depending on how the conversation might progress with any receptionist. Essentially, her plan would be that she was based in Cumbria and looking to move to Settle soon. No exact date was set but she believed within the next few weeks. She therefore wanted to register with a new GP. A friend of the family (she was thinking of Richard, Mike's Dad) had happened to mention a Dr Parker who he'd known from their days as medical undergraduates and had recommended him to her. At the same time, she'd dream up a recent medical condition that she wanted to get reviewed. She thought maybe something like a skin rash would be suitably vague. But would they buy it? There was only one way to find out! She rehearsed the mock conversation a few times first and worked through a few ways in which the conversation might progress.

And then she tried phoning the GP Practice! The number rang at the other end. One ring, two rings, three rings and then four ... and someone then picked up at the other end:

"Good morning, Settle GP Practice can I help you?" It was a female voice (no doubt the receptionist, Emma thought).

"Oh, hello," said Emma. "I wonder if you can help me. I live over in Cumbria but I'm looking to move into Yorkshire very soon – not far from Settle at all so I'm needing to register with a new GP. A friend of the family happened to recommend Dr Parker."

"Would this be as a private patient or through the NHS?" quizzed the receptionist.

Aha, thought Emma, the first curveball question, and she had considered that this might be asked! "Ideally" she said, "through the NHS – are there openings for new patients?"

"You're in luck, yes" answered the receptionist. "Can I have your name please?"

"Oh, sure", said Emma "Olivia Brown" (Olivia happened to be her middle name and thinking of Mike's last name she just decided to use a different colour). She felt that 'Olivia Brown' was suitably nondescript and would be sufficiently vague as to give no clues at all as to the identity of her real name.

The receptionist continued quizzing her for other details and she gave her actual address and contact details. Emma then waited for her moment. It sounded as if the formalities had been dealt with and so she spoke up.

"Only, I've got a medical condition right now and I was wondering if it might be possible to have a quick chat with the Doctor now, if by chance he's available?"

"Oh, I'm afraid not. Typically, you do have to be formally registered and then we'd need to fix you up with an appointment, even if that's just a phone consultation." She paused momentarily before continuing. "But presumably you do already have a doctor where you live right now? Surely you can contact your current doctor about your condition?"

"Oh, yes, I suppose so," said Emma. "I was just thinking I might try to kill two birds with one stone seeing as I'm looking to register with your practice anyway. That's not a problem. I guess that's what I can do."

Emma was cursing her bad luck as otherwise, she felt as if the conversation had flowed smoothly up that point and she felt almost in touching ground of getting to speak to and hear Dr Parker's voice. And then, a slice of impromptu good fortune occurred.

"Can you just hold a moment, please?" said the receptionist. At this point she heard the receptionist lower her voice slightly, but she could still make out what she was saying.

"Yes, I've just taken your coffee through Doctor, it's on your desk." And then, a male voice responded. "Thanks Cheryl. And can you send the next patient through, please?"

Emma was listening intently and from hearing those few words being articulated, in her own mind she was now convinced. Nick Rawlings was Terry Parker! She quickly hung up.

CHAPTER XVIII

Now Emma was very confused. She was convinced that Nick Rawlings and Dr Terry Parker were one and the same person. But why? None of this made any sense to her. It was one thing for someone to knowingly change their name for a variety of reasons, but to change their name while still retaining their old name (?) What would be the point? This also made her ponder whether this was directly connected to her own quest to find her genetic father. She also thought it somewhat unusual that the receptionist had also made no mention of Terry Parker's imminent retirement, as Nick had explained to her.

All her research, right from the first moment when she'd contacted the Fertility Clinic, up to the recent meeting with Nick Rawlings (or was that even his name, now?) was starting to take its toll on Emma. While she felt she'd made considerable headway in some respects, from another perspective she felt in many ways she'd gone full circle and was now facing another brick wall. She was now convinced that Nick was Terry. But then Richard, Mike's Dad, had also acknowledged knowing Nick as well. Maybe he was oblivious to Nick's shenanigans around his name change. Another flurry of possible avenues to explore entered her head. Should she get Mike to ask his dad if he knew of a Terry Parker now? She couldn't really see much point of making the trip across to Settle now, although she felt it would be fascinating to stand face to face with Nick again and ask him about Terry Parker. Of course, she still had Nick's email so she could always try emailing him again. He had been responsive in the past. Or should she now share all her findings with Mike and enlist his thoughts and help? She decided to send one more email back to Nick to discover what was going on, first. If no joy from that enquiry, she would summon Mike's support.

From: emmab@gmail.com
Follow-up enquiry.
To: raw@gmail.com
Hi Nick,

I just wanted to send you a brief note of thanks for agreeing to meet up with me last Saturday. It was lovely to chat with you. There is one query I'm trying to fathom out in connection with my earlier research. On the Edinburgh University alumni website there is a group photo I found where I'm sure I can see both you and Richard White. However, the name assigned to you appears to be 'Terry Parker'. Are you able to clarify this for me, please? Obviously, the picture is from quite some time ago. It's possible it isn't you, although that seems a little unlikely. Or maybe a mistake was made by the University, and you've been incorrectly assigned the wrong name somehow(?)

Thanks again,
Emma

She clicked send and waited. Would he even respond? Was it, perhaps a genuine mistake in the University records? Or maybe, just maybe, she'd uncovered some deeper, more sinister plot to conceal his real identity from her.

CHAPTER XIX

Terry Parker had just seen his last patient of the day. He was looking forward to finishing off at the practice to go home. Before doing so, he routinely concluded all the patients' notes, checked in with the receptionists to ensure there was nothing else outstanding to manage and make a final check of his emails. He was nearing the end of working his way through his emails when his phone rang. As he went to answer he recognised that it was Richard White who was calling him.

"Hi Richard, how's it going?" enquired Terry.

"Hi Terry. It isn't!" said Richard.

Terry could tell by the tone of Richard's voice that he was in a serious mode and that this was not a moment for any levity. "What do you mean?" quizzed Terry.

"It's Emma. She's just sent me another email. Somehow, she's tracked you down from that old University website. She found a picture with us both in it and she can see the name Terry Parker by your image. Terry, we've got a problem here. I suspect she now thinks that you and Nick Rawlings are the same person!"

"Well, we are!!! And what do you mean, *we've* got a problem here? This entire scheme was your idea from the start. I merely played along with you."

"Maybe" said Richard, "but I don't want to get bogged down in semantics here. Agreed, you bought into the plan, but equally, you were the one that eyeballed Emma and clearly told her your name is Nick Rawlings. Honestly, I'm not sure what to suggest for the best. Shall we carry on with the fiction?"

"Well, Richard. Given this development, maybe it is time to consider just telling her the truth. It would save on telling all these lies! Yes, it will be devastating, but is it preferable to doing a whole lot of sleuthing and finding out the dreadful truth on your own? Your own credibility would take a serious dent now, wouldn't it, should that happen?!"

"I'm not sure. Maybe we can still pull this off. She only has the photo to go on as far as we know. What if I simply don't respond to the email?" said Richard.

"Yes, but you've responded to the others she sent you, didn't you? Wouldn't she smell a bigger rat if on this occasion you don't respond?"

Richard remarked, "well, I'm not going to make a knee jerk reaction and respond to her straightaway. I need to mull this one over a bit. The two main choices would seem to be continue as we started, in which case we now need to think up a plausible reason for you having changed your name from Rawlings to Parker, or we tell her the truth. And when I say, 'the truth' I still mean the abridged version."

"How do you mean?" quizzed Terry.

"I still have no intention of telling her the whole story. We can still spare her the stress of that. No, I mean I could simply respond and apologise for having misled her about the name and that the man she met is in fact Terry Parker ... assuming you'd be okay with me confirming that ...?" Richard paused as if waiting for some agreement from Terry. "Okay" was what he heard from Terry, but it was said very slowly, almost as if he wasn't quite certain whether to agree and was, himself, cogitating.

Terry continued, "but how are you going to explain the reason for misleading her and the name change and all?"

"Well, that's not quite so troubling to me to be honest. Let's face it, there are so many scammers and nefarious individuals out there. It should be quite easy to rationalise the falsehood. I can just say it was a front used for a little initial 'protection' of my, sorry, I mean your, identity. Once you'd met each other I can say it was clear that she was genuine but given my need not to want to make it a longstanding communication channel that it hardly seemed the point to clarify the false name used. Ultimately, I still don't want to divulge the fact that it's me who's her genetic father. I don't know, something like that. What do you think?"

There was a short delay where he could tell that Terry was mulling it over. "Hmm, okay, yes, I guess so. I just sincerely hope she goes with it, puts it to one side and can just live with it. Although I was only with her for a short while, she's a nice young lady. I'd hate to think she'd be getting hurt by you not revealing to her the complete truth. Are you otherwise convinced that this would stop her digging any further and she'll just accept what you tell her?"

"That's the million-dollar question, isn't it Terry? I have no idea, but I can trust to instinct. Obviously, I'd be declaring a lie to her. You said yourself she's smart. Would this increase her inquisitiveness? If I'm lying once to her, would she sniff out any other doubts or uncertainties. I'd just have to hope she's satisfied. I'll still take a day or so to think this through before crafting a reply."

"Okay", said Terry. "I guess that's a plan. It doesn't sound like there's any plan that's going to be ideal given the circumstances. And of course, assuming you get past this hiccup you've still got the challenge of getting them to split up!"

"Yes, thanks for reminding me Terry" he said with a mild sarcastic intonation in his voice. "Don't worry, I hadn't forgotten that element. I was hardly likely to now, was I?"

"Alright, just leave it with me, Terry. I'll be in touch again in a day or two just to let you know what I've done, okay? And thanks again. I really didn't foresee this situation virtually taking on a life of its own. I hope I can still just nip it in the bud."

"Okay", said Terry. "Speak soon," and with that he hung up.

CHAPTER XX

Two days later, Richard indeed crafted his email response back to Emma.

From: raw@gmail.com
Re: Follow up enquiry
To: emmab@gmail.com
Hi Emma,
Thanks for your follow up email.
I guess it's time for me to confess to a little white lie here. Your research has been robustly conducted and, just to confirm, yes, you are correct, I am Terry Parker and not 'Nick'. In my somewhat weak defence, not knowing you from Eve initially, I was curious as to whether your initial contact was genuine or whether from a scammer of sorts. I have received odd scam emails in the past you see. We simply can't be too careful these days. Once I began with the pretence of being 'Nick' it was just easier to keep that pretence going – especially given I only perceived our meeting to be a one-off.

Again, I'm sorry for having misled you and hope and trust that you understand and accept this explanation – and apology.

Warm regards,
Terry.

Within minutes of sending the email, Richard again phoned Terry as much to keep him informed. He thought it was the least he could do given he was still, effectively, posing as Terry and he had disclosed Terry's real name in the email. Granted, Emma's sleuthing had already found Terry anyway but the fact that he was confirming as much by email felt the right and proper thing to do.

Emma read the email not long after it had arrived in her inbox. So, she was right with her suspicions! She felt a mix of emotions. An inner sense of satisfaction for having been proved right; a sense of anger and, yes, also, to an extent, of betrayal that Terry had felt the need to lie to her, and to maintain the façade during a face-to-face meeting. She wondered that, had she not pressed ahead with her diligent research efforts whether that lie would have lived on and she'd still be of the belief that his real name was Nick. All told she felt disappointed by the experience. She tried to see it from Terry's side as well, but she still felt that his stance had been something of an 'over the top' response.

Now that Terry had laid his cards out on the table, as it were, Emma felt that there was little more she could do. He'd clearly set out his own intention for this not to become a regular line of communication and the meeting was seen very much as a one-off liaison. She'd finally had the chance to meet him, and she was grateful for the fact that he did seem to be a pleasant, intelligent individual. At least she'd had that much. She supposed that his remark about upcoming retirement and relocating to the South Coast may also have been half-truths, but she suddenly felt as if these were comparatively trivial parts of the bigger picture now. Did she even care anymore?

Nevertheless, she felt that she was bearing the anxiety fully on her own shoulders. In a way she felt that she'd accomplished a fair deal and maybe now was the time to take stock and be prepared to move on with her life. After all, she'd managed to track down her genetic father, meet him and get to chat with him. All of that seemed a virtually unattainable goal just a few weeks earlier. Now she'd reached this significant milestone, she felt the time was right to share the episode with Mike. He'd at least be supportive, possibly quite interested, impressed even (?) and he'd be someone she could lean on for a little moral support. She felt she now needed someone to share it with.

It was the following weekend when she met up with Mike that she emptied her heart out to him. "Mike, I've got something I feel I should share with you," she'd said. She remembered seeing a look of worry appear on Mike's face. "Oh, it's nothing to worry about. Just that research I'd been doing into my parental origins. I didn't want to overwhelm you with all the minutia of details, so I spared you quite a lot and just kept it high level. But I've reached a point where I think I just need to move on now. Anyway, the guy I introduced you to in Costa ..."

"Yes?" said Mike, clearly interested in what she was about to share with him.

"Crazy as it might seem but ... he's my genetic father!"

"What?" exclaimed Mike. "You're kidding me, right?"

"No, it's true. I basically tracked him down through various routes and yes, it's him. You were probably right, by the way, when you thought he might have looked familiar. By some strange quirk of fate, he did happen to study at Edinburgh at the same time as your dad."

"No way!" said Mike, "but, well, why the heck are you telling me this, now ... why didn't you tell me when we were in Costa?"

"Oh, come on Mike. I could tell a few weeks ago you were only part interested in what I was sharing with you. It's not your dad we're talking about here, it's *my* dad. The 'dad' I've never known anything about, so I could tell it wasn't the same burning interest for you as it was for me."

Mike was silent for a few seconds, taking in what she'd said. "Well, I had absolutely no clue. You know what, you've done an amazing job to track him down. That must have taken some dedicated research. And the coincidence around Edinburgh University was a bit spooky, eh?"

"Yes, agreed," said Emma.

"So how did you get his contact details and stuff?"

Emma was now in her element and her voice took on an extra level of excitement and enthusiasm. "Ah, well," she continued, "that's where all my super sleuthing skills took over!" She grinned and she could tell Mike was now firmly interested. "Go on then, tell me more ..." he said.

"Would you believe I've had conversations with a local Fertility Clinic ... and actually visited them to find out more!"

"Really?" He laughed out loud, probably at the sheer audacity that Emma had demonstrated. "Well, how did you know which clinic to go to?" said Mike.

"Pretty easy, really. All the donors are kept on a national database," said Emma.

"Yeah but, isn't it all kept confidential?" quizzed Mike.

"Well, to an extent, I guess" said Emma, "but effectively I still have the right to be able to contact the donor ... depending on a few caveats and the like. It's amazing some of the stuff I found out. For instance, the law's been changing over the years effectively to make it a bit easier for people like me to be able to track down donors."

"Wow, that is pretty amazing! So what, they had his contact details? That must be tricky, especially given these records must have been started ages ago. I mean, people move around, relocate, some of their details get changed over time."

"Sure, that's true of course, Mike. Obviously, when he was up in Edinburgh, he had one address but of course now he's over in Yorkshire."

"What, and you managed to track him down from some lead up in Edinburgh? But he must have studied up there decades ago. How did you get a live connection?"

"You're right, Mike. Of course, those studies did take place a long time ago. I had an Edinburgh telephone number and an address up there, too, but when I phoned, yes, all I really discovered was that the address had been used for student accommodation. In fact, I spoke to the current landlord, so I suppose it's still being used for the same purpose today."

"But the landlord wouldn't have been around all those years ago at the place – would he?" quizzed Mike incredulously.

"No" said Emma, chuckling lightly, "although there's no reason why not. No, he'd been the landlord for around the last 10 years or so, but he did confirm that it had been used for student digs for many years before he took ownership of the place."

"But surely he had no idea about this Nick guy?" said Mike.

"Well, a couple of points there. No, the landlord I spoke to had no idea from all those years ago, but here's another thing I learned. Guess what? His name isn't really Nick!"

"What?!" said Mike. "He gave you a false name? For heaven's sake, why did he do that? And more's the point, how did you find that out?"

"Aha" said Emma. "Well, when we met up in Costa, I did believe that his name was Nick. We'd exchanged a few emails. But after I did some further sleuthing off the back of the fact that he knew your dad and studied up in Edinburgh around the same time I managed to find some student photos. I found one class image that showed your dad and 'Nick' in the same photo. Only his name wasn't listed as Nick. It was Terry Parker."

"What?" said Mike incredulously.

"So, I emailed him back with this new information I'd found. It just wasn't adding up at that point and I was really confused. He said all along that he wasn't interested in having any sort of longstanding communication between us going forwards and the meeting at Costa was set up as a kind of one-off meeting. Anyway, he responded back quite promptly, confessing to the fact that he'd kept this white lie going with me. He was certainly apologetic, but it sounded like he was worried about it being a possible scam." Emma paused for a moment. "Did you get that, Mike? Me, the evil scammer?!" They both laughed.

"So, let me get this right. He told you his name was Nick. Then you found a picture showing him as Terry. And then he 'fessed up because basically you'd caught him out?! Too funny. And weird! It all seems a bit cloak and dagger though. Almost like he might have had some hidden agenda. Something to hide, almost."

"Yes," said Emma. "It did seem strange to me. But he's been quite friendly and approachable otherwise and, well, you met him didn't you, albeit briefly? He seems an okay sort of guy, wouldn't you say?"

"I guess," said Mike. "So, just going back to how you tracked him down. That phone number and address up in Edinburgh effectively drew a blank, then? And you just had his email? So, without that you'd have just hit another dead end, yes?"

"Yes," confirmed Emma.

"Wow, that was pretty fortunate then, wasn't it? I mean, even an email could have changed given the length of time involved. All told, you were lucky."

"Actually, Mike, thinking about it a bit more, that's the one thing that's now confusing me a bit more."

"Oh, how do you mean?" said Mike.

"Well, at first, he told me his full name was Nick Rawlings and this also explained how his email was derived just taking the first few characters from his name."

"Right," said Mike. "And?" he added, clearly not yet fully understanding the point she was making.

"Well, his real name *isn't* Nick Rawlings, is it? It's Terry Parker! So, what he told me about how he thought up his email doesn't add up anymore, does it?"

"Well, are there some similar letters in his real name that would still correspond to his email? What exactly is his email?" queried Mike.

"No," said Emma. "I thought at the time it was quite an unusual sounding email. Just using the first three letters of his surname … 'Rawlings', so 'raw'. It added up once he'd explained it, but, like I said, his name's Terry Parker so 'raw' doesn't really make much sense any more, does it?"

Mike stared intently at Emma and his voice took on a serious tone. "Did you say his email starts 'raw'?"

"Yes" said Emma.

"What, 'R … A … W…?'"

Emma again, confirmed and spelled it out in full … raw@gmail.com.

"OH MY GOD!" screamed Mike. "OH MY GOD. OH MY GOD!"

"What, what is it, Mike?!" Emma was now feeling scared by Mike's reaction.

"Raw@gmail.com" he said in a slow deliberate tone, is my dad's email!

"What? No?!!!" said Emma, barely able to comprehend the full implications of what Mike had just shared with her. "But this is the email I got from the Fertility Clinic!"

The penny dropped simultaneously for both of them at virtually the same moment. There were only a few seconds before one of them spoke again. Their minds were fathoming the meaning of this new revelation. And then Mike said, "you know what this means, Emma? We might be related ... brother and sister!" He quickly corrected himself ... "well, half-siblings, to be correct!"

"No, no no!!!!" cried Emma. "That ... that can't be?" She started to weep ... "can it?" she quizzed incredulously.

"Well think. Let's just think this through calmly and logically. You got the email raw@gmail.com from the Fertility Clinic, right?"

"Yes, that's right," said Emma.

"That's definitely my dad's email!" said Mike.

"How come he has that email?" quizzed Emma.

"Simple," said Mike. "Those are his *initials*. His middle name is Alan ... so ... Richard Alan White ... 'R' 'A' 'W'. And I'm 100% sure that all emails are unique. In other words, it's my dad's email and it won't belong to anyone else. Although of course that doesn't mean he's the only person who could access that email, but you'd still need to know the relevant password. I can only think of two reasons why someone else would or could ever access the account – either by permission, or by being hacked! And why would you even want to share an email account with someone else? You just don't do that. And regarding the scamming thought, that's virtually a non-starter. To hack into someone's account and then create some elaborate communication pretending to be from someone else would be too crazy for words. That seems to imply that any emails you've been receiving have been from my dad and not from this Terry character at all! And we know that they do know one another, so, thinking this through logically, that maybe means they've been working in cahoots together – effectively to hoodwink you! What other possible reason could there be? But why?"

"I really don't know, Mike. But maybe your dad got my first email, realised what was going on and ... didn't want to hurt my feelings? But then that still wouldn't make sense. I mean, he knows we're going out together. He'd have realised the issues straightaway!" said Emma.

"Maybe" said Mike. "He's always been a good guy, so maybe that was his thought." But if all of this is true, and I can't think of any reason why it wouldn't be right now, what the hell are we going to do now?!"

Emma had stopped crying now. Her initial upset was being replaced by feelings of anger and anguish in equal measure. Mike's initial feeling of sheer confusion was also being replaced by other mixed emotions, some anger but also a profound feeling of curiosity and, naturally, anguish, particularly around prospects for their otherwise burgeoning relationship. Clearly, to them both, any thoughts of a continuing non-platonic relationship suddenly seemed to be dead in the water. It was fair to say they were both in a state of shock.

"We can't ..." Mike hesitated, trying to choose his words carefully ... "you know ... carry on being a couple. For a start, it'd be illegal, wouldn't it?"

Emma had started crying again.

"Emma, I'm just so sorry."

Between her sobbing, she stifled a mirrored response. "Me too," she said, "but it's not your fault. It's neither of our faults. I just can't believe this is happening. It all feels surreal."

"I need to have this out with my dad and truly get to the bottom of this," said Mike.

Emma quickly responded, "do you think that's a good idea, Mike?"

"Well, we need to know the truth. The whole truth here. And it seems like my dad is the one who'll have all the answers, wouldn't you agree?"

"Yes," said Emma, "I suppose so. Should we speak to him together?"

"No, he's my dad. Oh … sorry Emma, I didn't mean that to come across as insensitive as he's quite probably your genetic 'father' too. I just meant, well, I've grown up knowing him as my dad all these years. It might be best for me to talk with him myself in the first instance. Are you okay with that?"

"Yes, sure, if you think so. You should know him a lot better than me, after all. But when?"

"No time like the present. He'll be around later. I think it'll be best to tackle him on his own rather than when my mom's around. I'll pick my moment and aim to speak to him later today."

CHAPTER XXI

Four hours later.

Mike had arrived at his parent's house and was standing in the lounge looking through the window at the front garden. He could see his father drive up the approach, come to a halt, get out and walk the few yards to the front door. Although Mike no longer lived at his parent's house, he still had a key to let himself in at weekends when he visited. There was no one else at home as he knew his mother had gone out for the afternoon and wasn't expected back for at least another hour. Richard let himself in and, a moment later walked into the lounge.

"Hi Mike, how's it going?" It was meant as an informal pleasantry, so it came as a surprise when Mike responded, "basically Dad, it isn't!" The tone of voice used also gave away that Mike was clearly perturbed and had something serious on his mind.

"Oh?" quizzed Richard.

"Simple question, Dad. Have you been lying to Emma?"

"Lying to Emma?" he repeated, hoping for a brief second that this would buy him time to formulate a meaningful response. He knew, or at least guessed, straightaway, that the cat must well and truly have got out of the bag.

"Yes. I think you must know what I'm referring to. Or do I need to spell it out?" demanded Mike.

Richard reflected briefly on the fact that he couldn't recall a time when Mike had ever spoken to him in this manner before. At the same time, Mike hadn't specifically mentioned what this lie was about, and he was careful not to jump the gun, so he bought more time. At the same time, he didn't want to insult Mike's intelligence, so he probed with a clue.

"Has this got anything to do with my old colleague, Terry Parker?"

"Too bloody right, it has!" exclaimed Mike. Richard hardly ever heard Mike swear so he knew the topic was heavy with gravitas. He also knew that now was the time he'd basically have to come clean.

"Mike," he said. "Look, what can I say? Hands up, you, and most probably Emma, I guess, have been doing some sleuthing and have uncovered what is basically a terrible truth."

"But you knowingly concealed that truth from us … knowing how harrowing this would be for the pair of us!" Mike was clearly incredibly angry, but also appeared grief-stricken.

"That's true Mike and, sincerely, I am so sorry for that. But just know that I did have the best of intentions at the time, I was merely trying to spare you the anxiety and grief."

"So that makes it okay?" Mike didn't wait before continuing, "but you knew our very relationship would be decimated by what you found out, so how could you possibly think that would spare our anguish? As soon as we found out, you knew that'd be 'it' for the pair of us: the end of our relationship. Or did you have some other nefarious plan in place to prise us apart?"

"Mike, Mike, honestly, I had no idea what the next steps would be but yes, you're right, I guess I knew deep down from the start that you'd not be able to continue with the close relationship you have with Emma. I was taking one thing at a time. Maybe I was thinking you might just drift apart or something. I don't know. Don't get me wrong, Emma's a lovely girl and all that, but, well, since you went to University, I know you've been seeing rather less of each other anyway. You're both still young. You're mixing with different groups these days. Who knows how long you might have been together? Clearly, if the relationship was still looking strong then ultimately, I'd have felt obliged to step in and break the news to one or both of you. Please Mike, this came as a huge unforeseen bombshell to me, too!"

"How long have you known?" queried Mike.

"If it's any consolation, not long at all." Richard assumed that Mike would have been told about the emails that Emma had been sending so thought it now futile to spare him anything but the truth. "You'll no doubt be aware that Emma's sent me one or two emails. Again, when the first one arrived it was like a bolt out of the blue. I wasn't sure what to believe and genuinely for a moment, I did wonder if it may have been a scam of sorts. So that's how long I've known, just these last few weeks."

"And then you dreamed up this whole fictional 'Nick' character to pretend to be you?"

"Mike, it probably sounds a whole lot worse that it really was. You must believe me I was trying to spare Emma's feelings. Clearly, it's now …"- he paused, as if grasping for the right word ",,, backfired. Please believe me, I am so sorry for hurting her … and your feelings. I would never have knowingly wanted for that to happen."

"Well," said Mike. "It's a right mess, don't you think!" He paused again. "Does Mom know?"

"No", said Richard. "Just me and Terry, plus, of course, you and Emma now."

"It's really tough to think you not only concealed but also manipulated the truth and basically lied to her!"

"Mike, I know. I've said I'm sorry. I can't turn the clock back. If I could, I would, but again, my intention was never to cause either of you any pain. I know you'll be feeling sore right now. I just hope, in time, you can also see this from my angle too. Listen, do you want me to speak with Emma?"

"No!" he said, almost shouting. "Haven't you caused enough damage?" said Mike.

"I just thought it might be better if she heard a formal apology direct from me. Listen, again, I'm sorry. Just know I'm always here for you." And with that, he turned and walked out of the lounge and into his study. There was little more he felt he could say but maybe, he thought, Mike now needed time to mull and reflect on the situation. At least now, the truth was out.

About an hour and a half later Richard heard a gentle tap on the door of his study.

"Yes?" Mike popped his head round the door.

"I'm, er, going to get going. I've got stuff to prepare for tomorrow," said Mike.

"Oh, okay," said Richard. "What are your … plans, around Emma?"

"We haven't discussed yet but we will this week. We can't go on seeing each other … as we have been … obviously," said Mike.

"No … no, of course not. I do understand the er … predicament. Of course. Listen, I think it's only right your mom knows about this too, so I'll tell her later when she gets back. Okay?" quizzed Richard.

"Yes, sure. Whatever. Bye," responded Mike curtly.

"Sure son. You take care," Richard responded, trying to sound as sincere and as genuinely upbeat as he could muster. Mike turned and closed the study door behind him. Richard heard him make his way down the hallway.

He heard the front door open and then shut to. Not an easy situation, he thought, but hopefully the healing could now slowly start to take place and everyone could begin to move on.

CHAPTER XXII

Two hours later Sue arrived home. Richard had barely thought of anything else since Mike had left and it was clearly preying on his mind. He also felt that he wanted to let Sue know as soon as possible. No time like the present was one of his mantras. He could hear her walk down the hallway and guessed she'd headed for the kitchen.

"Hi Sue", he called out. "If you're fixing yourself a cuppa' can you make one for me too, please?"

An affirmative "Uh huh" was all he heard, somewhat muffled via the pathway to the kitchen from his study.

Several minutes later Sue appeared, carefully holding two mugs. "Here you are", she said, "remind me, whatever did your last slave die of?" They both smiled.

"Tell you what, let's go and relax in the lounge, I've got an update, of sorts to share with you," said Richard. Sue handed him his mug.

"Oh", said Sue, "not some juicy gossip from the village?"

"No, afraid not" said Richard as they both walked through to the lounge and sat down. "Although it is something quite, how shall I put it ... significant."

"Yes. It's not an easy thing to share really." He could see that Sue now wore a worried frown. "Nothing for you to fret about, as such, just, well, a somewhat unusual set of circumstances that have arisen."

"Now, I'm curious, Richard. What on earth is it?"

"Okay, so, you know when I was doing my medical training all those years ago in Edinburgh?" continued Richard.

"Yes," replied Sue.

"I probably mentioned to you before that I did a spot of sperm donation for a while. It was fairly common practice throughout the medical undergrad community. Well, I guess it's one of those things you do and then, forget about."

"Yes," replied Sue, now wondering where on earth Richard was going with this topic.

He continued, "well of course, the whole point of the process is to provide support to all those couples out there who are struggling to conceive, and you hope that you can be of some benefit to them. Who knows how many such couples might have benefited from what I did back then?" Richard realised he was in danger or prevaricating, so he brought himself back on track. "You see, any such recipients who go on to successfully give birth, well, those offspring apparently now have legal rights to be able to track down donors. Like me."

"Oh, good lord," said Sue, "and you've been tracked down by someone?"

"Yes," said Richard, "but this is where it's gets a bit spooky. Like I said, there's no easy way to say this but, it's Emma!"

"What?" responded Sue incredulously. "How can that be?"

"It's just the way it is. In theory it could, of course, be anyone. In this case, bizarrely, I'll admit, it just happens to be Emma."

"Well, are you sure?" said Sue.

"As sure as we can be," said Richard.

"Er, there's something else I should also share with you," said Richard.

"What?" quizzed Sue, "isn't that bad enough?" Richard could tell she was becoming emotional, but he couldn't tell whether it was more surprise or anger, or maybe just a mix of both.

"When Emma starting to make her enquiries, she obtained my email. I wasn't even aware that the authorities were allowed to divulge such information, but, well, it's been a bit of an education for me, Sue, to be honest. The legal system in this country has changed you see since I was doing the donor stuff. I mean this was a few decades ago. Anyway, she emailed me, though, of course, my identity wasn't exactly revealed by my 'raw' email. Consequently, when the penny dropped as to who she was I was initially loath to reveal my identity. I was hoping, somewhat foolishly with hindsight, that I could keep my identity concealed. Clearly, there was no way Emma and Mike could, well, you know, continue with their relationship as is. So, I did something maybe a bit stupid. But I really thought it would help."

"What?!" said Sue.

"I was just trying to help. I mean, to alleviate the anxiety for Emma. It seemed like a good idea to continue to hide my identity, so I didn't divulge my name when she contacted me. The thing was, she then asked if she could meet up with me! Of course, that was the last thing I wanted, so I convinced my old pal, Terry to pose as me. Only we, well, I came up with a ruse to say he was called Nick Rawlings."

"Nick Rawlings?! But Richard, wasn't that just a crazy idea?! What on earth was the point of that?"

"Don't you see? That was a way of covering my email?"

"What?" said Sue.

"Think about it ... my email starts 'raw' ... so that could be the start of Nick's last name."

"But he's not a real person!"

"No, of course, I know that, but this was just going to be a one-off meeting and then it'd all be done and dusted." He paused briefly … "only sadly, it wasn't!"

And maybe, with hindsight, I reckoned that if I could convince her that I'd agree to just that one meeting – and then make out I didn't really want to have any further ongoing communications with her, that she'd appreciate my position and that would be that."

"Yes, but …" Sue continued, "she'd still be going out with Mike!"

"Yes, yes, of course, I knew that. I was already thinking about that second part of the conundrum. I hadn't worked out a specific plan to tackle that thorny issue. But, as it transpired, it was all pretty much academic anyway. Terry did meet up with her – in Costa in town and it seemed like that part of the plan was working simply fine. But then Mike bumped into them both!

At the same time, Emma had been doing some more digging through some old records at Edinburgh University and found a picture of me and Terry. So, she smelt a rat, put two and two together and … well, that then opened a little can of worms. Mike confronted me earlier today. He was, understandably, angry. Once Emma got chatting with him, he learned that Emma had emailed me and of course, he immediately recognised my email address!"

"You fool, Richard!" said Sue, as she then started to weep.

"To be fair, it's so easy to be wise after the event. It all sounded quite plausible to me at the outset. There's no way I could have foreseen how this would play out. How was I to know that they'd have bumped into Mike of all people? I mean, what were the odds of that happening? But for that, this could have turned out completely differently. Sure, we'd have still been left with the dilemma of how to handle Mike and Emma's relationship, but ...". He paused a moment before continuing. "But yes, of course, you're right. I can see you're upset, Sue, but we can't turn the clock back. It is what it is. At least it's all out in the open now. Mike and Emma are sensible people and I'm sure now both fully understand the predicament, hard though that may be."

He felt he needed to state the situation in simple terms. "But yes, Mike and Emma are, in effect, siblings. Well, half siblings. They both carry my genes."

Sue continued to weep, grabbed a tissue, and ran from the room. He heard her quickly go upstairs and, presumably, into the bedroom. While he was empathetic to the dilemma and to Sue's feelings, he felt that her reaction was probably a little over the top and maybe as much down to the sheer shock of what he'd told her. He thought it best to allow her some time on her own.

A few hours later, with Sue not having returned downstairs he decided to go to bed. The light was out in the bedroom, and he could see that Sue was, seemingly, fast asleep. The next morning, conversation was stilted to say the least. Richard thought it prudent to just allow Sue some time and space to mull things over.

CHAPTER XXIII

L ater that same day, Sue arrived back home after having been out for several hours. Richard was again in his study. He got up and went into the hallway. "Hi Sue" he said, keen to start a cordial conversation. "Hi" she said. "I was just about to make a brew. Do you fancy one? I thought it might be good to chat."

"Oh, sure" she said, "but I suppose there's not really much more to be said though, is there?"

"Well, you know what they always say, it's good to talk." Richard smiled in the hope of drawing out a reciprocal smile from Sue. He succeeded. Just.

Several minutes later Richard brought through two mugs of tea and handed one to Sue. "So" he began, "you've had some time to consider the, er, issue. Any more thoughts?" quizzed Richard.

"Not too much, really. I wondered if maybe they'd made a mistake at all," said Sue.

"A mistake?" responded Richard, with an air of incredulity to his tone. "How do you mean?"

"Well, all these organisations are run by people with their various systems and processes, aren't they? And with so much reliance on humans, there's always the chance for human error to creep in, isn't there? I mean, can you be absolutely certain that their records are accurate?"

Richard felt that Sue really was grasping at straws and, under normal circumstances he'd have shot her down immediately, but, given the circumstances, he paused a moment to gather his thoughts for a more conciliatory response. "Yes, I see what you're saying Sue and of course, you're correct, there is always a possibility of a mistake having been made. Though, to be fair, I'd feel that would be highly improbable."

"Even so," continued Sue, for something so serious, there'd be no harm in checking, would there?"

"I suppose. But I was a donor all those years ago and ultimately, Emma tracked me down via the email they had on record for me," countered Richard.

"Yes, granted," persisted Sue, "but we're assuming that your ..." she struggled for the right word here ... "donation ... was correctly assigned to your record ... your name and your email."

"Well, yes, of course," said Richard.

"So, like I say, although it might seem like a total long shot, wouldn't it be at least worth some sort of checking?"

"But surely, they'll just go back through their records and find everything matches up," said Richard.

"Richard", Sue paused for a little dramatic effect. "You've got nothing to lose in simply trying though, have you?" She didn't pause long enough for Richard to respond before continuing, "anyway, I was actually thinking more along the lines of, oh, I don't know, a DNA test or similar. That way you're not checking the clinics records but more of an independent test. A bit like a cross check."

Richard was slightly amazed at Sue's thought processes here. What she said made clear logical sense, even if he had no doubt at all that he was Emma's genetic father. But to appease Sue, he found himself nodding in agreement with her suggestion.

Sue still found a reason to continue with a parting shot. "Just think Richard. If there *was* a mistake made by the clinic, however remote a possibility that might seem right now, could you *ever* live with yourself for not having explored that avenue and finding out for certain? Think of *those* ramifications!"

"Well, when you put it like that, I suppose, no, there's every reason to exhaust such a possibility. It still feels a bit like clutching at straws, but …" Richard tailed off without bothering to finish his sentence. After a lengthy pause, he said "thanks Sue. I really mean that. It might be a total long shot, but, as you say, what's to lose by finding out for certain?"

CHAPTER XXIV

Around the same time.

E mma had continued to struggle with the dilemma she'd faced. This left her totally uneasy about her relationship with Mike. Would it be simplest to just end the relationship or was there any useful mileage in continuing a platonic friendship (?) She still hadn't decided what to do for the best. But she had made two decisions. First, considering it all she decided that, at least for the present, it made sense for both her and Mike to have their own space for a while. She'd called him the day after they'd last met to suggest that to him and he had agreed. Second, she thought it appropriate to update her mom. No doubt this was going to be as much of a shock to her as it was to Emma. She had chosen her moment to have this discussion on a Saturday morning after breakfast. Her Dad was out for the morning, and it was just the two of them sat in the kitchen.

"Mom", she'd started. "You know when I was asking about who my biological Dad was?"

"Yes," replied her mom.

"Well, I started carrying out some research online. And I was able to contact a clinic that provided me with more information."

"What?!" said Linda.

Emma guessed that her mom would be surprised, and possibly a little annoyed, to learn that she'd been continuing to dig after their earlier conversations on the topic and so she was somewhat prepared.

"Yes Mom. If you remember, there was little you were able to share with me, remember? So, I still had some unanswered questions. I quickly found out that it's possible to track down details about donors. And ..." she paused a moment, "I did so and obtained some updates."

"Only, what I found out was pretty bizarre to be honest."

"Oh?" said Linda, a worried expression now appearing across her face.

"You're not going to believe this mom, but Richard White's my biological father!"

"What?!" cried Linda. "No, no, surely that can't be!! Oh no! NO!!!"

Emma could tell this was a sledgehammer blow for her mom, but she felt there was little point in pussyfooting around the subject.

"Are you sure, Emma? Are you certain? Could it be a mistake?"

Her Mom almost sounded as if she was in a denial cascade. "Oh Emma. That's tragic ... what about Mike? Does he know ... and Richard?"

"Yes, Mom. I was given Mike's Dad's email as the official donor contact. It's a long story but it's true. Mike knows. We chatted about it a few days ago. We're giving each other some space while we think it through, but basically, yes, we're related."

"Oh, no, Emma. That's awful for you!" and Linda immediately moved across to Emma to hug her. They both started to cry.

After several minutes when the sobbing had subsided, Linda spoke again. "And does Sue know? And do they know that I know, too?"

"No idea, Mom. Though I guess sooner or later, yes."

CHAPTER XXV

The day after Richard and Sue had spoken, Richard called Mike by phone to let him know what they'd discussed. In particular, he was keen to broach the idea of getting a DNA test done on himself and Emma.

"Mike, is that you?"

"Yes, hi Dad."

"I wanted to catch up with you briefly. Okay to talk for a minute or two?"

"Yes, sure," said Mike.

"Only, I wanted to let you know that I told your mom about recent events. As you'd expect she was shocked to say the least but, at the same time, she did have a good idea. She suggested we carry out DNA tests ... on me and Emma. I appreciate this might sound like a slightly strange thing to do and that maybe there's little point, but, as Sue said, it'd be a good way to make sure. I was going to reach out to Emma direct, but I wanted to just check with you in the first instance. What do you think?"

"I guess you're right, Dad. I am thinking though, really ... is there any point?"

"Well, I remain unconvinced myself, said Richard, but, as Sue pointed out, there's always the chance a mistake could have been made. This would be one way for us all to make absolutely certain, yes?"

"I suppose so. I guess we've nothing to lose by trying."

"And how do you think Emma might be about this? Do you want to mention it to her first?"

"No idea Dad, but yes, if you want, I can let her know and get back to you, okay?"

"Thanks son, oh, and of course, it goes without saying I'll naturally cover the costs of these tests myself. That's the least I can do. Keep me posted then, okay?"

"Sure Dad, will do." And with that Mike hung up.

CHAPTER XXVI

Mike texted Emma to simply say, 'can we talk, briefly?' Emma had responded an hour later with 'Sure, when?' Two hours later Mike called Emma.

"Hi Emma, how are you keeping?" was his opening line.

"So, so," she responded.

"I wanted to quickly catch up and provide a quick update."

"Okay. By the way, I told my mom about what happened."

"Oh ... and ... how did she take it?"

"How do you think? She was in shock. Just like I still am!"

"Anyway, the main reason for calling you is because I had another chat with my dad. Incidentally, he's also told my mom and, probably like your own mom, she too is distraught. However, she did come up with a suggestion and, while I don't think it will change anything, it's still an idea."

"Oh, what?" quizzed Emma.

"A DNA test!" said Mike.

"What for?" said Emma.

"Well, like my dad said, it'd be a way of kind of double checking what you've found out. People can sometimes be prone to making mistakes. A DNA test is pretty quick and simple to do, and it'd be another way to remove any doubts."

"I don't know. What's involved?"

"Oh, they're really straightforward. You just take a swab from inside your cheek and send it off for testing. My Dad said he'll pay for them to be done. No harm, eh??"

"Okay, I guess. There's nothing to lose. Just let me know once you've found out some more, okay?"

"Sure Emma. Hey, and take care!" With that, the call ended.

Mike quickly texted his dad to update him.

On receipt of the text from Mike, Richard prepared to order the DNA testing kits. With his medical connections he was remarkably familiar not only with the process but also the various options. He could have arranged for a visit to a clinic for the test to be administered, but he felt more than comfortable simply ordering the test kits for self-administration. He also felt that this might prove somewhat less intrusive for Emma. He wasn't sure about this, but he was just following his gut instinct.

Several days later, the kits arrived by registered mail to his home. Even for those unfamiliar with the process, each kit came with clear instructions as to how to obtain the buccal cavity swab. He emailed both Mike and Emma to let them know that the testing kits had arrived. He still felt somewhat awkward having any direct contact with Emma at this point, so he suggested Mike drop by to collect the kit to hand to Emma the next time they met up. Within an hour, Mike had responded to Richard's email, also copying in Emma to say he could collect the kit 2 days later. Sure enough, 2 days later he popped in during the early evening. Richard and Mike exchanged pleasantries, but he could tell that Mike was only interested in collecting the testing kit so that he could hand it over to Emma. Richard gave him the kit and suggested that he get

Emma to get her swab taken and then he could add that to the return package that would also contain his own swab. Mike agreed to do so and pop back a couple of days later.

Two days later, true to his word, Mike returned.

"Hi Mike".

"Dad. So, Emma took her swab and it's here in this envelope".

"Great," said Richard. And with that, he located his own test kit and, over the next minute or so, in front of Mike, he proceeded to take his own swab. Once taken, he inserted it into the bag provided and placed it inside the same large envelope as Emma's, before firmly sealing the top. "No time like the present, Mike, if I get a move on, we can just catch the evening post. I was just going to walk round to the post office. Want to join me?" It was only around a 10-minute walk from Richard's house. He was hoping to get a few minutes together with Mike where they could have a quick catch-up conversation, but he could tell that Mike wasn't really in the mood.

"No, it's okay, I need to get on actually. Things to do, people to meet. But hey how long will this take before the results come back?"

"Not sure," said Richard. "Pretty sure I read something about 10 working days in the enclosure. But as soon as it comes back of course I'll let you know. Er ... would you and Emma want to come round here so we could open it together?"

Mike was quick to respond, no doubt having already broached this with Emma himself. "No, I already asked Emma about that, and she said she'd prefer to find out the results herself, on her own."

"Oh, okay, in that case I think it might be best to include a note to that effect then." With that, he re-opened the envelope and went over to his desk. In what seemed like less than a minute he had quickly typed up a brief letter outlining the request for the results to be addressed separately to both him and Emma, printed it out and added to the envelope before re-sealing. They both walked through the hallway and through the front door.

"Right Mike, like I say I'll let you know as soon as I get something back, ok?"

"Okay, bye" said Mike as he made his way to his car. Richard started to walk to the post office and, 15 minutes later, the package had been handed across the counter and sent on its way by recorded delivery. Now they just had to wait.

CHAPTER XXVII

E mma had had a while to reflect on the entire situation. She had been generally out of sorts, although she had continued to focus as much as she could on her studies and her swimming continued to provide something of a release of energy for her. At the same time, during her reflections she still found herself ruminating on the sheer incredulity of what had happened to her, and she was still thinking long and hard as to how many other unfortunate IVF offspring might find themselves in a world of uncertainty as to who their genetic parents were. Although she was finding her mind going in circles, she eventually came to a conclusion, of sorts. While no one could deny how unfortunate the situation had become for her, she had a desire for something benevolent to come out of it. She struggled coming to terms with the thought and it was difficult to comprehend how something practically beneficial could come from the situation but then it hit her. She would find a way to tell her story, in the hope that it might help shed light on what had happened and maybe even provide some support for others finding themselves in potentially similar situations. But how to go about doing this? She was unsure but remained determined to explore the best way of doing so. Maybe, just maybe, this could also provide some cathartic release for her, too.

A few days later she began a fresh conversation with her mom on the topic. Her first thoughts were two-fold. First, she wondered about approaching the local press. She felt her story was possibly quite unique, although the wider issue of the challenges of tracking down genetic donors was probably a much more widespread issue for many. Her second thought was around approaching her school. Given her areas of study, the thought occurred to her that her current dilemma was very closely related to the joint disciplines of both biology and psychology, and she wondered if she could use her recent experiences to form the basis of a project that would also have a very personal element.

She found her mom was very empathetic to her ideas and, perhaps, just a little proud that she'd come up with such a creative way to exploit what was essentially, a tragic occurrence in her life. "Emma," she'd said, after a while. "I honestly don't know how you managed to come up with such ideas. I'd have imagined most people would want to just brush it under the carpet and forget all about it. It's very laudable how you're trying to look for something positive out of all of this. Maybe, though, work on the school project piece first and spend a bit more time thinking about going to the local press, okay?"

"Sure, Mom. Thanks for being here for me."

True to her word, a week later, Emma had approached her personal tutor at school to broach the subject as a project to span across biology and psychology. Her tutor had been incredibly supportive and felt it was not only a good idea but also one with such a unique angle. Emma had already gleaned a certain amount of information from trawling the internet, contacting the fertility clinic, and generally learning about the donor process. Her tutor had advised her to think about the specific objectives and purpose of her project, but other than that, she felt she'd been given the green light to proceed with the project. For the first time, Emma felt a glimmer of hope that something vaguely positive was emanating from the horrible situation that had befallen her.

CHAPTER XXVIII

12 days later

The DNA test results package arrived on Richard's doormat. In fact, Sue was the first person to see it lying there, along with a couple of other items of post. One looked like a utility bill and the other was some promotional advertising material from the local DIY store. She pondered for a moment as to how the truly important items of post were seemingly always amazingly easy to distinguish these days. Richard was in the kitchen. "Richard" she shouted through from the hallway, "I think that DNA result might have just arrived! Shall I open it?"

Mike appeared in less than 5 seconds. She could tell he was keen to assume authority in wanting to open the envelope first himself. "No, I'd like to open it myself, Sue, if you don't mind."

"Sure," said Sue and she handed him the envelope, retaining the other two for herself to open. She could tell that Richard quickly switched on a true laser focus of concentration. They both walked into the lounge as Richard was already tearing open the seal. Inside were what looked like several pages all folded over once to fit snugly inside the C5 sized envelope. Richard unfolded the papers and began reading the top sheet. Sue remained there, just a yard or two away, silent, watching Richard's every eye movement and facial gesture for a clue, however minor, that would tell her what was in the letter. After several seconds, she could bear the tension no longer.

"Well?" she said, 'what does it say?'

His face took on a slight grimace, an expression not of contentment or satisfaction, but of some dawning realisation of the facts. And then he spoke. "It's true" he said. "This confirms me as Emma's genetic father."

"And it's unequivocal?' quizzed Sue.

"Yes," he continued. "In the small print it basically states that there's a greater than 99% probable match in gene commonality between me and Emma."

Sue had turned half away from Richard to stare out of the lounge window. For a moment she didn't speak.

Richard continued to speak, as much to himself as to Sue, she felt. "To be honest I felt we were grasping at straws to expect any other outcome here." He sat down on the sofa, with the letter still firmly in his grasp. And then, it was as if his mind was analysing all the pieces of the puzzle. After a short while, he spoke again. "Do you know?" he said, "when I was discussing some of the details with Terry, you know, after he met up with Emma, he was telling me how he was desperately looking for any additional clues that might help to additionally convince Emma that *he* was her genetic father. He was cute, you know. He picked up on the ability to roll your tongue, like this ..." and at this he quickly stuck out his tongue and rolled it. "Terry's also able to roll his tongue like that and Emma quickly discovered that she could too. Plus, he also picked up on her cute facial dimples. He'd tried to suggest she might have inherited that nuance from her mom, because, sadly, Terry is totally deficient of cheek dimples, but of course ... and he paused to smile, both me and Mike are also blessed with that trait." He paused to reflect a moment. "And now, all the pieces of the jigsaw have all come together. All doubt's been removed."

Sue had remained quiet, listening to Richard's analysis, before she spoke again.

"But surely you're not the only person with facial dimples who can also roll your tongue like that!"

"No, of course not ... but ..." he trailed off without finishing his sentence. "But it's all pretty much irrelevant now."

CHAPTER XXIX

I
t was less than an hour after he'd discussed the DNA results with Sue that Richard sent a text message across to Mike asking him to call as soon as he could as he had a further update for him. Mike rarely received messages in such format though he regularly checked his social media account and was quick to acknowledge and respond to Richard. It transpired that he was in the vicinity, so he asked if it'd be an idea to pop in. Richard saw his reply and replied affirmatively.

Less than half an hour later, Mike was at the front door.

"Hi Mike, come on in" said Richard and, together they walked into the lounge and sat down. "You're probably wondering what I have to share. First though, do you know if Emma's received her DNA results yet? Mine arrived this morning."

"No" said Mike, "I haven't spoken to her today. I was hoping she might just call me once she had them to hand. Maybe I can try calling her later today. Why do you ask?"

"Okay," said Richard, "well, just to confirm, mine arrived today and the results show, much as we anticipated, that I am Emma's genetic father. I just wanted you to hear it from me first."

"I'm not sure if Emma's seen her results yet," said Mike.

"I can talk with her if you'd like?" said Richard.

Mike was quick to respond. "No, no, I'll talk to her. It's perhaps best if it comes from me. And besides, it gives me the opportunity to reach back out to her."

"And," Richard replied, "how exactly is the lie of the land between you two, right now?"

"We've hardly spoken to each other since this all kicked off, which I totally understand from her perspective. But I'd like to think that, once the dust settles, we can at least continue to be friends and at least remain civil to one another. It's still taking a while to properly sink in that we're siblings – well, half-siblings I suppose."

"I'd better get going," said Mike. "I'd like to get in touch with Emma. If she's got the results and looked at them, if nothing else, I'd like to at least be there for her." With that, he got up and made to leave.

"Sure, Mike," said Richard. "Like I say, I'm so sorry it's all come to this. There's certainly no way I'd have envisaged things would have taken a turn as they have done. None of us could have predicted any of this. On one level at least this DNA result provides a bit more finality. I nearly said closure there, but that term's become such a cliché these days. Good luck when you do get to speak to Emma. Let me know how it goes, okay?"

"Yes Dad. Will do." Mike exited through the front door.

As Mike got to his car he sat in the driver's seat and looked back at the house. His Dad was still in the front doorway. He lifted a hand to wave goodbye, and he saw Richard wave back before then closing the front door. He reached into his jacket pocket and retrieved his phone. He immediately looked up Emma's number and made the call. It rang a few times and then he heard Emma's unmistakeable voice at the other end.

"Hi Emma. Mike Here. Just wondering how you are?"

"I'm okay. Is that all you called to say?" she quizzed.

"No. Actually I was wondering if you heard back yet on the DNA result yet."

"No, not yet. Nothing's come back yet. Why?"

"Only, I've just been at my dad's. His results came through today and he just shared them with me."

"Hang on," said Emma. Mike could detect that Emma was in motion with some muffling and a hint of some other conversation going on in the background. After several seconds Emma spoke again: "okay, I can speak now. I was just in the kitchen with my mom and dad. I'm upstairs now. So go on, what did the results show, just confirming what we already know?"

"Yes, effectively," said Mike.

Mike could hear her start to sob.

Mike broke the silence. "Look, at least we've got confirmation now. If there was even a slight doubt before, that's now been removed." Emma still wasn't speaking so Mike decided to cut the call short. "Listen, I'm still here for you if you want to talk more about this. I'll leave you to it for now, okay? Keep in touch." With that he ended the call.

CHAPTER XXX

The situation between Mike and Emma remained cool and the dawning realisation for both was that their relationship, as it had been, was effectively at an end. Mike busied himself with his own studies and some swimming to keep his mind occupied. Emma for her part did her best to focus on her studies as best she could.

However, on reflection she remained keen to want to do more. She remained eminently conscious of the fact that significant numbers of individuals perhaps faced a similar dilemma to her, certainly in terms of wanting to track down their genetic parentage and facing any number of challenges along the way. She found herself thinking back again to the sheer numbers involved for people working their way through the IVF process. She felt sure that that process itself must be quite troubling for many people, quite aside of the resulting progeny who simply may not always be aware that they're even the result of such a process.

Consequently, she found herself revisiting the statistical details about IVF, the numbers involved and reading more about the plight facing some people affected in this way. Her focus of attention reverted to her earlier thoughts, that her situation was somewhat unique, and the newsworthy perspective came back to the fore in her mind. She therefore reached out to one or two local newspapers to get their attention in the hope they might be sufficiently interested to allow some news coverage of her situation. She also approached her local radio station with the similar idea in mind. A little to her surprise, she received potentially favourable responses from one of the local newspapers and from the local radio station and, in the weeks that followed she found herself in communication with a local sub-editor and a radio broadcaster.

Ultimately, she soon realised that each of these media outlets appeared, at least superficially, to be genuinely concerned as to Emma's predicament and her quest to further raise the profile of the situation for people finding themselves facing somewhat similar scenarios. At the same time, she also became aware of their ulterior motives. At the end of the day the newspaper was looking for a newsworthy story. After all, their job was to sell editorial. Similarly, the radio show was looking for ways to enhance listening figures. That said, Emma felt somewhat heartened that her own story here was clearly being perceived to be of sufficient importance to garner their interest. The unusual twist with her own experience also lent to the general appeal. A journalist did meet up with Emma to get the details of her story and take her photo and her story appeared in the Westmorland Gazette a few weeks later.

The local radio station also invited her along to the recording studio and, for Emma, it made for an interesting diversion from her general day-to-day life of studying. She took part in a live interview combined with an opportunity for listeners to call in with any questions, around the same time that the newspaper editorial had appeared. She felt a little self-conscious appearing live, a little daunted as to what sort of questions the radio presenter might pose to her, but she found her to be warmly welcoming and reassuring. She also briefed her regarding any live questions that might arise from callers to the station and, as it was, there were only a handful of questions that did occur. In the main, the callers were very praiseworthy of her efforts to bring attention to the topic.

Inadvertently, this also raised Emma's profile at school and, in the months leading up to her final A level term she did collaborate with her form tutor and arrange to deliver a presentation to her entire school at one of the main morning school assemblies. Emma found that this experience was somewhat more daunting than either the newspaper editorial or the live radio interview. This was in part because she was thrust into the realm of public speaking which was not an area in which she had gathered any prior experience. In addition, the fact that she'd be facing such a large group of, essentially, her own peer group, also added to the pressure she was feeling. Also, she wasn't presenting on a topic of general interest. This was a topic that was hugely personal to her, which only served to add to her sense of anxiety. However, after a few practice sessions with her tutor, who helped her craft her presentation and guided her in how best to present her material and story, the day arrived, and she managed to carry it off to the best of her ability. Certainly, it was very unusual, at the school, to even be afforded such an opportunity. It certainly did no harm to her academic efforts in general in the eyes of her teachers and, somewhat to her surprise, when she finished the presentation, she was met with loud applause from all in attendance. She felt genuinely quite touched and emotional at the end and struggled to retain her composure. Her tutor and several other teachers lent their support and provided ample praise for her efforts that day. Similarly, her main class members also heaped praise upon her, many being otherwise completely unaware of what she'd been through in recent months.

Later that day, during her lunch break, she was making her way back along one of the main school corridors and, some way ahead, she could see another female student approaching from the opposite direction. They made eye contact with one another from being some 10-15 metres apart and, as they got closer, Emma could sense that this other student was heading straight towards her. She could see that she was starting to smile at Emma and Emma felt herself reciprocating. She recognised her as a fellow A level student although she was sure that she was in the year below Emma. She fancied that this girl was simply going to congratulate her for her earlier presentation. She was quite tall, similar in height to Emma and with shoulder length fair hair. They both slowed their walk and Emma could now sense the other girl was about to speak to her.

"Hi", she said, "you probably don't know me, but I'm Sarah. I'm in the year below you. I heard your presentation this morning. I thought it was very brave of you to do that! It was great and I wanted to say well done. What an amazing story!"

Emma found herself relaxing and immediately thanking Sarah for her comment. "Thanks for that. Yes, it's been a bit of a roller coaster ride to be honest, but I was pretty nervous this morning."

"Really" said Sarah. "Well, it didn't show. I thought you did a great job."

Sarah continued. "Listen, I don't know if we could maybe chat together sometime?"

Emma had instantly warmed to Sarah and was certainly amenable to meeting up with her for an informal chat. "Sure" said Emma, "was there anything specific you had on your mind ... I mean about my presentation?"

"Yes" said Sarah. At this, Emma suddenly flinched slightly inside. Sarah's tone had suddenly taken on a more serious demeanour and Emma looked intently into Sarah's eyes, wondering exactly what Sarah was about to say next as myriad thoughts cascaded through her mind.

"Like you, I'm also the result of an IVF procedure."

"Oh", said Emma, immediately feeling that, at the very least, she'd be able to provide a supportive shoulder for Sarah to lean upon. But Sarah then continued with an utterance that stunned her ...

"And I think there's a chance we might be related."

ABOUT THE AUTHOR

Alex Knibbs was born and bred in Birmingham, UK but he has also lived in Saudi Arabia, the Netherlands and the US.

He spent 20 years in training and training management within the pharmaceutical industry and, more recently, has become an accomplished Solutions Consultant.

His literary experience has been something of a love hate relationship. At school he struggled in English lessons taking 4 attempts to pass his O level. In later life he blossomed, taking in stints as a freelance physiology research newsletter writer (Peak Performance) and as a puzzle compiler. His interest in amateur dramatics and Toastmasters International also saw him writing press releases for various local newspapers. In 2004 he published his first book, 'The Claim Game', a light-hearted but informative account of his time spent as a personal injury claims manager for Claims Direct.

'Relative Uncertainty' is his first novel.

Outside of work he still likes to keep fit, having run marathons and competed internationally for the UK Life-Saving team in his youth.

Printed in Great Britain
by Amazon